A Sky So Close

A Sky So Close

Betool Khedairi

TRANSLATED FROM THE ARABIC BY
DR. MUHAYMAN JAMIL

PANTHEON BOOKS NEW YORK

*This is a work of fiction. Any resemblance to
persons living or dead is entirely coincidental
and unintentional.*

Translation copyright © 2001 by Betool Khedairi

All rights reserved under International and Pan-American
Copyright Conventions. Published in the United States by
Pantheon Books, a division of Random House, Inc., New York.
Originally published in Lebanon as Kam Badat al-Sama' Qareebah!!
by The Arab Institute for Research and Publishing, Beirut, 1999.
Copyright © 1999 by The Arab Institute
for Research and Publishing.

Library of Congress Cataloging-in-Publication Data

Khedairi, Betool.
[Kam Badat al-Sama' Qareebah!!. English]
A sky so close / Betool Khedairi.
p. cm.
ISBN 0-375-42096-7
I. Title

PJ7842.H685 2001   892.7'37—dc21   00-049164

www.pantheonbooks.com

Book design by M. Kristen Bearse

Printed in the United States of America
First American Edition
2 4 6 8 9 7 5 3 1

To my mother, and to my father,

so untimely our separation . . .

A Sky So Close

1

My memories pulsate up from the pavement as the street glides beneath our feet. The autumnal colors of the wall surrounding the school brush against your shoulder as we pass by each day. You'd always park by the baby palm tree on the corner, and from there we'd walk. I struggle to keep up with you, waddling like a female penguin. You hurry, holding my little hand, leading me to the place where I'd be taught how to walk with elegance. This morning Mummy told me— I'm sorry—I meant to say "my mother"—told me that they would teach me how to walk, how to sit, and how to dance.

How you'd argue with her when she insisted that I be taught there. I have no say in these arguments. I don't even know which language I should use. I'm only a small child, the top of my head barely reaching the level of your belt. All I have is my braid, which swings between my shoulder blades. You warned her so many times not to cut it, not to restyle my hair the way she wanted it. She likes it short and practical, but you want to watch it grow. You bend over to hug me goodbye, leaving me a small wet kiss in my ear. I wipe it away with my fingertips as you turn to go away. Your long strides take you past the row of palm trees which parallels the school wall, their thick trunks swallowing you out of my sight. Each palm tree you go past makes you seem smaller, biting a piece off you, as you recede in the distance. I wave to you, then I turn around and walk under the lofty archway decorating the school entrance.

I make my way through the big playground. Its wide pathways make the open space seem so much bigger. A group of boys in shorts are standing where two narrow corridors meet. The screams of another group of children reach me from the upstairs classrooms. Three girls walk down a path leading to I know not where. Their conversation is too grown-up for me. As they take the first turn to the right, they disappear; their conversation turns with them. I want to follow them, but I don't dare. I follow your instructions, waiting for the bell to ring. I hadn't realized that I was standing right underneath it. I take two steps back. I'm now standing with my back to the wall. I look around me. I see a teacher carrying a musical instrument bigger than me. The students go in. They come out. Nobody pays any attention to me. I feel like an ant.

They all carry bags, instruments, and hats. I watch them, frozen in this spot I've chosen. I play with the tip of my braid. In the corner on the left is a tap in the center of a circle of damp grass. As I look at it, I glimpse a bead of water; it glimmers in the sunlight as it drips from the spout starting to fall. Half a second later, the door of the classroom in front of me bursts open. The children rush out shouting and shoving, like a wave of dolls crashing into each other.

They look like tens and tens of twins, all wearing the same uniform. Their shoes are all similar. Their socks are all the same length. The ribbons in their hair have all been tied the same way. They're all of about the same height, and they're all, as a group or as individuals, much bigger than me. I join in their noisiness from afar. They've started throwing apples in the air above their heads. They kick at each other; dust rises around them. Their shouting gets louder with the chaotic movement.

Suddenly the bell above my head rings. I'm startled by the sound plus the strangeness of my surroundings. A stout woman emerges. Her frame blocks the entrance to the teachers' room. Someone shouts, "Miss Melvina is here . . . the religion teacher!" She's come to take me with her. Looking up, I hold in my frightened breaths. Over my head I see the huge signpost; I know that the sign says SCHOOL OF MUSIC AND BALLET. I've come here to learn how to read those letters. How large they are! I hesitate as I place my hand in the teacher's fat one. But I know that you won't be back for me until the day is done. They'll deliver me back to you when the bell rings again.

That first day at school was my first experience of time, trapping me between two long rings of a big scary bell.

The grown-ups ask me:

—How old are you?

I hold out the fingers of my left hand and my right index finger. I bring my hands together.

—Six.

I count them again to make sure I've got it right, then I always say:

—Khaddouja is also six.

—Who's Khaddouja?

—She lives near our farmhouse. She doesn't go to school because she has no shoes.

I believed then that children who didn't have shoes didn't go to school.

In that vast expanse everything was bigger than me. Even the way you looked at me, across the breakfast table, when I called my mother "Mummy" instead of calling her "Youm" or "Yumma" in the Arabic way. I only felt I was my true size when I was with Khadija; this person was the only creature in the world who made me feel that there was something, or someone, as small as me. I made her even smaller. I called her Khaddouja—"Little Khadija."

She was my world. She was everything that came in the second half of the day. A world that spread between our farmhouse and her father's hut, by the banks of the Tigris River, in our little village twenty miles south of Baghdad. Zafraniya, it was called—"Land of Saffron." That was where the apricot trees grew. Vast acres of graceful trees, their upper branches entwined. When the sun starts to sink over the apricot farm, their shadows fall as complex patterns of light and shade on the ground underneath. The youthful branches stretch out in all directions. Their sharp twigs seem like fingers, entangled in handshakes, exchanging bunches of white flowers. Each spring I wish that the flowers would last forever.

When the trunks of the apricot trees secrete a dark sticky glue, the color of a slightly burned syrup, we run to pick it. The gum is wedged between the rough folds of bark. We spend hours collecting it, kneading it into a ball as big as our fists. We press on the rubbery dough and roll it in the dust to make it less sticky. We stamp on it, flattening it; then we each take one end, pulling hard. We play a brief tug of war until the middle bit weakens, breaking in two. We share, making bracelets, rings, and hoops, which we hang from our ears. Sometimes we make false nails, trying to stop them from sticking together when we shake hands as we play "visiting the neighbors."

I watch Khaddouja sculpting her doughy gum into the shape of a fish or a bird. She adds two pebbles, one on either side of the creature's head, giving it colored eyes. Watching it all the time, she lifts it high above her head as she runs around, weaving through the low-hanging branches. She doesn't tire of hovering in the air with her bird until she bumps into one of the trees and falls backward, laughing at the giddiness that overcomes her. The sticky bird falls into the ditch.

After our toys lose their bounciness, the apricot gum melts in our hands. Time trickles through our fingers, colored like burnt honey—a sign that this magical day with Khaddouja will end. The sun is setting; my mother is waiting for me at home. I must leave my wild, skinny, childhood friend, who awaits my return from school every Thursday. She hides by the big farmhouse gate. Neither one of you notices her there. Her people call us "the doctor's family." I later found out that they call everyone who has a car and lives in a house that's not made of mud a "doctor." They also called us something else. They called us "the foreign woman's family."

My mother was relaxing on the black sofa in her room. She was wearing a black dress. The whiteness of her skin stood out. It was as though her face, arms, and legs were made of porcelain. She looked like an imported Chinese miming puppet. A rag doll strewn on the sofa. She was listening to the BBC World Service. A fashion magazine and a booklet about slimming lay by her side.

On the low table where she has propped up her feet is a small bowl filled with hazelnuts and a musical cigarette box. Every time she opened it, it played a tune. How I hated that tune! What you hated was the fact that she smoked. You thought it was improper for women to smoke. So you chose a separate bedroom, at the other end of the corridor, to get away from her clouds of smoke. She leans over to pick up one of those small colored bottles with the unusual tops. She will varnish her fingernails when she has finished trimming and tidying them. The nail file, tweezers, and scissors are in her lap. She hardly notices me entering. I greet her:

—Hello, Mummy.

She answers me in an English as white as her skin:

—Hello. Where have you been?

She's expecting my reply.

—Outside, in the farm.

As usual, she flies into a rage. The bowl of hazelnuts gets knocked over as she leaps up.

—You mean you were with that dirty little girl again. Didn't I warn you not to mix with that lice-ridden child?

—But Mummy, she's my friend.

She scolds:

—No! She's not your friend, she will only give you her diseases.

She starts to pick up the scattered hazelnuts, then asks:

—Did you eat anything when you were with her?

I answer in a low voice:

—Only a small piece of bread with some cheese.

She erupts again:

—My God! Haven't you seen how her mother uses dried cow dung for the fire with which she bakes the bread? Haven't you seen the hordes of flies that swarm around that cheese they make with their filthy hands?

I try to object:

—But Mummy—

Interrupting me, she raises her index finger, holding it up rigid and still:

—I'll speak to your father when he gets back. I'll make him stop you from going to the farm again.

I realized that I was going to be the cause of their next argument, but then, most days of the week seemed to be just another installment in a never-ending argument!

I couldn't understand why you shouted at each other so much. My going to the School of Music and Ballet made you throw pieces of your temper in her face just before breakfast.

—The girl will be spoiled!

She answers you from the kitchen:

—But the schools out here are so deprived. I want my daughter to learn languages, dancing, and socializing. I'm not asking for much.

You mimic the way she speaks:

—Dancing and socializing, not asking for much! But one day, she may pay too high a price for your decision.

She comes to sit at the table.

—I won't let her go to a primitive school!

Your face turns red, as if you were choking on a piece of dry bread.

—Don't you realize, woman, that we're now in the Arab, Islamic world, and she and I are Muslims? This education, which you are calling "arts," could damage her future prospects.

—It would still be better than damaging her morale in your local girls' schools. She's showing promise and talent. Why do you want to keep her in isolation? Isn't it bad enough that she mixes with that Gypsy girl and those illiterate fools who spend the whole day running around in that disgusting farm?

—Woman, you're talking about a culture you don't understand. I've warned you about the differences we'd face in raising her. I know what I'm talking about, why don't you listen to me?

—I listened in the past, that's why we didn't send her to nursery school at the age of four like the other children, because we're so far away from civilization. But now I'm sick of this isolated village and its primitive people. The time has come for her to be educated in the city. I want her to go to school in Baghdad.

—Woman, let her mingle with the peasants' traditions, there's no harm in that. Let her bond with the land, with the people and their animals, the way we were raised. For God's sake, let her see what you can't see!

My mother calmed down, then replied:

—I know that we can't afford to buy a house in the city at the moment; I have no choice but to wait until your projects and commitments in this area are done. I'll also overlook my loneliness, which you seem to have forgotten as a result of your numerous engagements. But I will not compromise with her education. The discussion is over. OK?

How often your arguments ended with that single word. From you, or from her.

The days pass. My mother announces that she hates the apricots because they give her an allergy. They give me Khaddouja, who comes over with all the gossip about the families who live in the mud huts built on the riverbank. In spite of your conflicting plans, you were unable to stop my mother from sending me to that school. And she in turn was unable to convince you to forbid me from going to the farm. Your disagreement allowed me to mingle with both worlds. Just like our house, which was in itself two worlds.

Once again, I join Khaddouja. We spend the entire afternoon looking for earthworms and snails. We turn over the stones and pebbles, pouncing on the insects sleeping underneath them, some on their tummies, some on their backs. We gaze at the ants with their glimmering sheen as they slip in—out—in—out of their lacy, sandy mounds. We stamp on their anthills; how we laugh as we watch them scatter. The snails end up on the liquid gum that oozes out of the pores of the apricot trees. We spend hours collecting those fragile jellied creatures that were languishing peacefully in their helical shells, and attach them, with pleasure, to the tree trunks. Khaddouja entices them out by singing to them a peasant's rhyme in her hoarse voice to coax them out of their hiding places:

> "Oh, snails, snails, show us your horns, oh but . . .
> Snails, snails, come out and start to head butt . . ."

The naïve molluscs respond to her appeals. They extend their small heads from their safe havens, their feelers flailing at the air. They clamber onto our hands as though to kiss our sweaty palms. They leave behind them a thin transparent strip of sticky slime. It tickles; we laugh even louder. At the end of the day we find our pockets full of snails that haven't succumbed to the charm of our song. I ask Khaddouja:

—What shall we do with all these snails?

She answers without thinking,

—We must kill them!

She beckons to me; I follow her immediately to the tree we call "the Punishment Tree." Khaddouja believes that the snails are defying her; she has to punish them without any hesitation. We head toward the tree which produces more sticky gum than any other in the entire apricot farm. We stick all the snails we still have onto its trunk until it is completely covered with all kinds of insects and other creatures, punished as decreed by Khaddouja's laws. We crush the ugly ones; they burst open under our feet, leaving behind a wet mosaic of shattered shells and grayish fluids. Khaddouja sneezes suddenly and small white petals from the flowering apricot tree descend gently upon our heads. In the distance we hear my mother calling.

Father, why didn't you let that night pass peacefully? Did you have to fight with her because of the way she washed her hair? I, too, could never understand that peculiar habit of hers. For some strange reason, my mother would always wash her hair at the kitchen sink. She's just finished washing the dishes. She rinses the sink twice with boiling water, then bends over. Her long hair flops into the metal basin, its weight settling on the silvery surface as she exposes her long white rubbery neck. She turns on the tap; the water flows onto the mounds of hair that lie there. She scratches it with her nails. Scratch, scratch, scratch. It must have been the sound of the scratching which upset you. The way you would get upset when someone squeezed powdered starch between his fingers or cut a piece of foam or a sturdy sheet of cardboard with a sharp knife. Screech, screech, screech. Why do we suddenly quiver when we hear an unpleasant scratching sound? I can never bear to hear the sound of a fingernail passing over a sheet of paper or a wooden surface. My mother can't stand it when I make a sound as I grind my teeth. Gizz, gizz. Or the crackling sound from my knuckles when I forcefully bend my fingers backward. She shouts at me "Stop it!" her face twisting into an expression of obvious disgust.

That's exactly what happened when you went up to her and shouted:

—Stop it!

She answers calmly from underneath the veil of hair.

—It's alright, I've cleaned the sink.

—It's not a question of cleaning the sink! You rinsed it with boiling water to get rid of the grease from the dishes so that it wouldn't cling to your hair. But did it ever occur to you that the hairs you shed might block the drains? What is this infuriating way of washing your hair? It's not hygienic and it's discourteous.

The rubbery neck turns around to where you're standing. My mother has made an opening in her hair; she looks at you through it,

—I'm sorry, but I've never managed to get used to your way of bathing. Using a small bowl that floats in a huge cooking pot full of hot water! You sit on that ridiculously low wooden stool, and the water goes cold before you've finished! I'll bathe the way I want to and I'll join you later.

We exchange a knowing glance; I follow you to the sitting room where the television has been left on. The evening's entertainment has started. My mother has missed the first five minutes of the English film that she's been eagerly awaiting. She soon joins us with her long wet hair coiled into a bun. We all settle into our favorite seats to watch the film. Ten minutes pass, then you make the first sound, click. You've picked up your worry beads in the middle of the film and begin running them through your fingers. Each bead drops down onto the preceding one with an agonizing slowness, click. Then after a little while, again, click. This time it was her turn to say "Stop it!" That was the start of another argument. You exchange angry words. The comments become more heated, the phrases more cutting. Many loud noises fill that pitifully small space inside my ear. I find myself hiding behind the sofa. My braid comforts me. I tickle my neck with its tip as you do with your shaving brush. A minute later the shouting from your seats gets louder. I stick my braid in my ear. I wish I could say "Stop it!" to the two of you.

The next day, Friday, the Muslim day of rest, was no calmer. My mother started the morning complaining continuously; sometimes uttering words I didn't understand. She puts her hand down between the folds and the cushions of the sofa, retrieving your white cotton handkerchiefs, which you insist on using when you have a cold. How many times she's begged you to use the paper tissues that she calls "Kleenex," enunciating each syllable when she pronounces the word. But you insist on spitting into your hankies. You then stuff them down the side of whichever seat you are using at the time. It was her misfortune that you always forgot them there. Getting them out was one of her chores. She'd allocated a big red pot for them, to differentiate it from her other cooking pots. She used it for the disgusting weekly task of boiling your hankies. She boiled them in soapy water with a small amount of bleach to dissolve your mucus and saliva. When the green-grass-colored stains disappear, she picks up the hankies with a big pair of wooden tweezers. She rinses them in cold water and dries them before ironing out their creases. What a topic to start the conversation with at the breakfast table!

My mother has toast with jam and butter. You chew on a small piece of brown khubuz—our local round, unleavened bread. You are waiting for one of the peasant farmers to bring over the thickened cream they make. She never allows me to have any, because of what she calls "those strange black spots" on its surface. I hold my breath as I watch your hand movements. As you lift your cup of tea, she lowers her cup of instant coffee. You put on your glasses and frown as you peer at the little black and white television, which is silent. A local comedy, *Under the Barber's Shaving Blade*, plays out soundlessly. The repairman couldn't make the barber's assistant, Abossi, speak. My mother lowers her copy of the *Times*. It's several days old, but she has only just received it. Finally, the phone rings, the tension is shattered. After a little while I make my escape, heading out toward Khaddouja.

Today is a holiday. We'll go to the very edge of the farm, where the barbed-wire fence surrounds it. Inside it is another fence of thick weeds with thorny ends. There's no avoiding their sting. We cut our fingers and knees on their blades as sharp as razors. Khaddouja had set up a swing for us between two palm trees. Her older brother Hatem tied the seat—a basket which Khaddouja's mother had woven out of dried palm fronds—to the trunks of two adjacent palm trees with a heavy rope. We take turns; Khaddouja lets out several hoarse cries of joy as she clambers onto the flimsy seat. She clings tight to its edge and wobbles on our primitive plaything. Then it's my turn. I kick the air with my feet . . . I rise upward . . . I kick harder . . . I'm framed in the milky blue. All the palm trees are below my two bare feet . . . the sun is swimming in the waters of the river. I spread out my toes . . . pencils of light pass through the four gaps between them. With my other foot I kick even harder . . . I rise higher toward the heavens . . . I breathe in the horizon . . . then . . . A sky so close!

As I tremble on our swing, Khaddouja wanders around awaiting her turn. She looks for her favorite wild plant. She parts the weeds with her little hand, picking a fresh herb. Its long stalk is wrapped around itself. The locals call it Sheikh Smalleh. She peels the herb with her fingers. It resembles a thin green banana. Khaddouja doesn't know what bananas are. I found that out when I was describing them to her. She peels off the green shoots exposing the herb's slim core, which is like a moist purple hairy sheaf of wheat before it has dried. She throws away the peel and puts the purple pulp in her mouth. She chews on it as I watch her from the swing. Her image is far, near, far, near. Suddenly the rope breaks. I'm lying on the ground on my back. The basket seat of woven palm fronds is underneath me; Khaddouja is on top of me. She cries, "Where's Hatem?" I repeat after her, "Where's Hatem?" We can't put the swing back together on our own. We have to look for him.

A dusty path winds its way between the fields. The farmers' sons gather there on holidays. They usually meet on Fridays, having made their escape from the farm through an opening in the wire fence. They push and shove each other, tripping on each other's feet, on the hem of their dishdashas—their long loose cotton garments—or on a shoe that has lost its heel. We observe them quietly. When their overactive limbs calm down, they start exchanging their colored glass marbles, rubber slingshots, and little boxes of gunpowder. If one of them has been lucky, he'll have a brand-new wooden spinning top. When they finish bartering, Ubaid, Khaddouja's cousin, cries out, "Come on, let's go to the beer factory!" They all barge toward the large building adjoining the farm. The place is usually bustling with activity, but today the group of boys sneaking into the area doesn't arouse any attention. We follow in their tracks, some distance behind them, eager for another adventure.

We choose two large barrels to shelter behind and watch the boys' world from afar. They've sat down in a circle on a wide wooden pallet, where workers stack crates to transfer on forklifts. The five boys have squatted down around a pile of brown bottles with the word "Ferida" printed on them in large white letters—the famous Iraqi beer. The bottles had been thrown onto a pile of rubbish due for incineration.

The boys delve into the mound, coming up with the damaged bottles they need for their game. Each one of the boys takes his turn and lifts a bottle high in the air, holding it by its narrow end. With his other hand, he makes a warning sign to the other boys before he throws the bottle down onto the hard ground. It smashes into tiny pieces; all that remains is the round tip of the bottle neck. The boys all start clapping, encouraging each other, "Well done the lion! Welcome, fearless!" They gather around, examining the fragments to determine if the bottle has been broken correctly, according to their standards. The rules of their game are that each boy should obtain the neck tip of the bottle he has broken in the form of a neat round ring so that he is able to wear it without cutting himself. They wear their glass rings on their fingers to demonstrate their prowess in the game of smashing the bottles, their favorite challenge. The undisputed winner is the first one to wear five glass rings, one on each finger. His prize is the largest piece of mastaki-flavored sweet from the tray of Ammu Jasim, the traveling vendor who covers the industrial estate by the rural road leading to Zafraniya.

Before the game has ended, the group's mischievous fool Hassoon, who is the youngest of the boys, has fitted a ring of broken glass from a bottle top around his little penis, which has sprouted suddenly from beneath his dishdasha. He holds it up with his left hand through the cloth, and, using his right hand, crowns it securely with the glass ring. He creates a little bulge that stands out in front of him. He shouts out to the others, "Who can do what I've done?" The boys start laughing insanely. Hassoon asks them again, "Who can wrap his thing in a little turban?" The boys run toward him as he dances around. When they head off, they leave their wooden pallet behind. It's now covered with tiny bits of broken glass that glint in the sunlight like sugar crystals. We've forgotten all about our swing, but then Khaddouja remembers her delicious herb, saying, "Come on, let's chew on the Sheikh Smalleh."

That was how I spent my days with her—a series of Fridays, each one different from the others.

———

OUR HOUSE, or rather what your colleagues at work call the Expert's House, has rooms where voices intermingle. Your deep voice that resembles your dark skin—somebody once asked you if you borrowed your skin color from the Indian market—mingles with my mother's high-pitched tone. When she becomes upset, it sounds like the whistle of a boiling kettle, releasing its anger as the steam spits from the spout. I inherited from you the exaggerated darkness of my skin, but I had to wait until my sixteenth year before I was sure if I'd inherited her vocal talent. She'd often sing excerpts from *Rigoletto* while she bathed or *Carmen* while she dusted the furniture. When she cooked, her favorite songs were black jazz classics. Sometimes when she was really depressed she would hum tunes from the Second World War, but she'd swallow the words and their notes as soon as you came in. It was obvious how annoyed you were by her domestic singing activities. To avoid any comments that might lead to further arguments, she'd abruptly cease her humming, as if she'd closed her mouth around an ice cube and was waiting for it to melt.

I, too, learned this avoidance game, by constantly re-
minding myself not to mix the two languages when I spoke.
I knew how easily that could set off sour notes that would
reverberate around the house. How I hated to be the cause
of that day's battle, like the time I said:

—Mummy, give me a plate and a "spoon."

As I said the word "spoon" in my mother's language, I
noticed the snarl coming from you. I quickly repeated my
request. This time I asked for both the plate and the spoon
in Arabic.

On another occasion, I made the mistake, while talking
to you, of saying the word "door" in English. You were
about to leave the room. I said to you:

—Baba, please don't close the "door" on your way out.

You glared at me, then slammed it hard.

One day at the breakfast table I asked:

—Are we having "eggs" this morning?

You stood up and left the breakfast table without saying
a word, leaving me confused. The turning point was the
time I used the word "yellow," asking my mother,

—Mummy, do you know how to make "yellow"
kubba—those oval balls of boiled saffron rice, stuffed with
meat, like the ones Khaddouja's mother makes?

Her face reddens.

—Did you eat yellow kubba at their place? Did I not
warn you?

Your anger reaches a peak; you strike the dinner table
forcefully with your fist:

—First of all, they're not called yellow kubba, they're
called Aleppo kubba; secondly, what is it that you've been
warning her about? Not to mix with those who will teach

her how to speak her own language correctly? See how confused she is, how she hesitates when she wants to choose
her words. Have I not asked you time and time again to remind her to speak only in Arabic? When she leaves, she
says "Bye-bye" instead of "Salam." Whenever she meets
someone, all she says to them is "Hello" instead of "Mar-
haba." Why can't you teach her to say "Shukran" instead of
"Thank you?"

You continue:

—This child is going to become a laughingstock. Let her
mix with them freely. The time has come for her to express
herself in a way that can be understood. That is the least we
can offer her!

It was then that I realized how I could maintain my
meetings with Khaddouja. I learned how to mix my words
in a way that suited me, and more important than that,
I learned when to do it. Never when you were in a bad
mood with my mother, but when I wanted to join my friend
out in the farm, I'd intentionally mix the two languages.
Sometimes, however, I'd get muddled. My teacher once
asked me:

—What does your father do?

I answered:

—He shouts when my mother sings, and goes out a lot.

She laughs. She reminds me of the multicolored laughing cow on the box of French cheese. Her shoes are ugly
and green with bulky heels, which everyone calls "tank-
style." Her name is Miss Zuhour—"Flowers"; she teaches
us geography. I prefer calling her Miss Geography, teacher
of Zuhour.

She repeats her question, adding:

—What a cute answer. I meant, what does your father do for a living, not how does he behave. In other words, what is his job?

I answer her slowly, choosing my words cautiously this time:

—He's a trader in food flavorings.

I had no idea what any of those words meant at the time; later that year I learned that a trader was someone who bought and sold things. The next year, I learned that the word "flavorings" derives from "flavors," and your room abounds in them. Smells, fragrances, tastes, colors, powders, fluids, sweet vapors, and others that are acidic. They all emanate from small cardboard boxes, paper cubes, metal cylinders, transparent bags and dark-colored ones. They are interspersed with desiccating agents, samples in plastic containers next to weird and wonderful glass vials. You bring them back with you every day; they accumulate on the shelves, on the table that has no room for any more, and even underneath the bed. My mother can't understand how you're able to sleep where the air is loaded with the smell of sweets. She says that every corner of your room gives off a sticky aroma. You mutter, "It's better than the smell of nicotine." I think only of the ants that multiply, getting fat amid those containers. How could I get rid of them? With soap and water, or with an insecticide spray?

Khaddouja lives in several houses at the same time. She moves between her relatives, who live in three huts that lean on each other like the people inside them. When she takes me there, it seems to me as though the rooms can't contain them. They crowd each other underneath their low ceilings. But what really takes up the cramped space in those simple lodgings is the women's overgenerous abayas—religious black cloaks that cover their heads and bodies, competing for room with the men's wide dish-dashas. They take off their belts and hang up their garments on rusty nails on the back of the door, or rather a large piece of corrugated iron which is supposed to be the door.

The three mud dwellings at the river's edge present an image of forgotten structures. From afar one might think they were trivial, nothing; but to me they were everything. I watched the family build these huts. They used large empty tins which had held animal ghee, lining them up in neat rows and filling the gaps between them with mud and straw. They sealed off the corners with cans that had once contained powdered milk, other empty containers, and pieces of scrap metal. When a piece of dried mud would flake off the wall of one of these huts, I could read the words NIDO MILK or see the distinctive face of the pretty girl on the empty canister of vegetable oil. Those dwellings were the family's humble possessions; they had every faith that the huts would protect them from the heat of the midday sun and from the winter's rains. It was here that they received any strangers who might wish to mingle with them. And it was the thought of mingling with them that filled my mind, even though I never felt like a stranger when I was among them. They called me "the foreign woman's daughter," but they still welcomed me in any hut I chose to enter. Khaddouja would furtively tug my hand, or gently push me from behind, until I became accustomed to stepping inside. I no longer needed her encouragement—"Come on, come on, don't be shy."

As for Khaddouja, her entering our house was at the top of my mother's list of forbidden acts. She called her "the filthy lice-bearer." The more she refused to accept Khaddouja, the more I longed for the second half of the day, when I would encounter her brown face on the dusty track, halfway between our house and the river. Later someone will sprinkle the track with water. The water droplets will lie between the ridges of the track, clinging to each other like beads of mercury insinuating themselves into the soil through its pores. Khaddouja appears. Her squirrel-like face is tanned; the angle of her mouth is cracked and fissured. Her cheeks are discolored by the harsh sun. She leads me to her domain. We squat beside her mother, who is washing their pots and pans in the turbid waters of a nearby ditch. Her name is Delleh—"Arabic Coffee Pot." She prepares a stew with okra and tomatoes for her husband, Kadhim, Khaddouja's father. Everyone will gather around the metal tray when the food is served. The farm laborers eat their lunch late in the afternoon. They tear up the large flat khubuz and pass the pieces around to each other, making sure that Khaddouja gets her share of the meal.

I watch them until they finish their meal. Then Delleh comes toward us holding up two rings of simeet—round rings of half-baked dough encrusted with sesame skins rather than sesame seeds. We wear them as bangles on our wrists, proudly displaying them for a brief moment. We then devour them hastily before visiting the eldest person in their family group. She is an old crone in her eighties; everyone calls her Hijjia, the lady pilgrim to the holy city of Mecca. I call her Bibi, which means "Grandmother." Every time we go to see her, she laughs, saying, "Ha, you naughty ones, have you come to visit Bibi Hijjia?" We join her as she leans her humped back against the mud wall. She sits on the floor with her legs crossed, her worn-out worry beads in her hand. She scratches her head through her futa—the black veil covering her hair—with her yellowed fingernail, and re-positions the pin that holds it in place. Her posture and the way she sits are unchanged by the passing of the seasons. The overcrowded wrinkles on her face resemble the jagged fissures in the mud wall behind her. Indeed, her face is a condensed image of the cracks; Bibi Hijjia appears to be merely an extension of the wall. Her nose is most unusual. Her nostrils flare and contract with exaggeration as she tells us the story of the mother goat and her two baby goats, Jinjil and his brother Janajil. The mother leaves them on their own in the hut, for she fears the wicked wolf, then goes out to get them some food. She warns them not to open the door to anyone until she returns, not to be fooled by any stranger's voice, and to open the door only when they hear the secret song that the wolf doesn't know:

> *Jinjil and Janajil*
> *Open the door for Mum*
> *Milky in my udders*
> *Grassy in my horn*
> *Open the door for Mum.*

We're enchanted by the tune; we never tire of it. Bibi Hijjia finishes her tale, then asks her granddaughter to fetch the bronze bowl. We know then that our visit must end soon. The old woman starts to comb what hair she has left. She uses a wooden comb that has teeth on both sides. She dips the comb in the bowl of water and unfurls her white braids. She performs this ritual in total silence, in complete contrast to the vitality of her tale. We quietly make our way out of her room, leaving her to her reveries. On one occasion I made the mistake of telling my mother when I returned home that Bibi Hijjia had combed my hair with her wooden comb. It was as if I had announced the end of the world. "Jesus, the lice!" she cried. She didn't stop scolding me until someone advised her to wash my hair with kerosene. She stopped me from visiting the mud huts for two weeks after that episode. I spent the entire first week trying to get rid of the smell of kerosene that lingered in my hair, and in my bedroom.

There's always a first and a last time for everything!

In this case, the thing happened to be a necklace of white flowers. I sat with Khaddouja in the afternoon shadows under a row of bitter orange citrus trees. It was their flowering season. We've gathered the moist blossoms that fall from the trees this time every year. We pierce them with a threaded needle, making fragrant chains. I run back with one of these flower necklaces for my mother; I leave it for her on her favorite sofa, a surprise for her to find later. I go up to my room to get more thread before rejoining my friend in the citrus grove. As I come down the stairs, I hear my mother greeting her friend Millie, who always comes to visit us accompanied by her brother David, maybe because she doesn't drive.

Millie and David are English. They both work for a petroleum extraction company based in the large southern city of Basra, close to the oilfields. Whenever they come to visit their friends in Baghdad, they drop in on us in Zafraniya to see my mother. How her mood and tone of voice change as she welcomes them! She calls me over to greet them, asking me to shake hands and say hello in their language. I mutter the words as I gaze at Millie's ears. They're so minute, like two delicate seashells placed precisely on either side of her head. Everything about her is small in size—her shoulders, her hands, her feet. If we exchanged shoes, it would probably be a perfect fit! But David, who you, Father, insist on calling by the Arabic version of his name, Dawood, usually greets my mother with kisses; that makes you furrow your brow.

My mother's friends exchange kisses between men and women. Among your friends, it's only the men who kiss each other on the cheek when they meet. The foreign women tend to avoid exchanging kisses, restricting themselves to a cold distant embrace, whereas Arab women exchange numerous warm kisses, cheek to cheek. They ask where you are; I can see the reaction in their light-colored eyes when she answers, "He's at work, of course." I ignore David's attempts to embrace me, looking for my precious necklace. He has sat on it, uncaringly crushing the fragile flowers with his weight. Millie reaches out, offering me a piece of the usual gift she brings my mother, a sweet pastry they call "the flies' cemetery." They always laugh when they say its name. This scene is repeated every time they visit us. I can't understand why the merriment is reenacted time and time again. The dish itself is merely thin layers of a doughy pastry generously stuffed with black raisins.

I ask David to move so I can be sure. He stands up away from the sofa, brushing back his blond hair with a hand as white as my mother's. When they shake hands, their fingers seem to blend together in their whiteness. The cushion is covered with petals that had been ripped away from the thread; small yellow grains the color of egg yolk have been ground into the cloth. David smiles; his eyelids hide a sharp look that is directed at me. My mother says, "Don't worry, the farm is full of citrus blossoms!" He leans over, saving a single blossom that has remained unscathed. He picks it up from the cushion, very quickly brushing it with his lips in a smooth movement that is hardly noticeable. He then lets it slip from his fingers; it comes to rest in my mother's pink pocket on the left side of her chest. I have a strange urge to kick him and run, but, as if he'd read my thoughts, he quickly says:

—I'm sorry! I didn't notice your pretty necklace.

From this day on, I will never give another necklace of bitter orange blossoms to anyone other than Khaddouja.

My mother starts recounting her woes to her visitors. She complains about how filthy the road is, cutting its way through the farm that connects our house to the huts on the banks of the Tigris. All along the side of the road are piles of waste and rubbish. What she forgets to say is that it will all be used as fertilizer. She then tells them how annoyed she becomes when the water supply is cut off for lengthy periods, or when the electricity is cut off, sometimes for the whole night. She can't understand how people can sleep on the flat roofs—a normal habit in this country—or in the open air, listening to the frogs croaking. The three of them exchange cigarettes and expressions of amazement. I'm taken aback at how similar their hand movements are. They all turn their heads in the same way, saying "Oh," "Aha," and "Really" with every other sentence.

My mother offers them weak tea, as usual, but they still add milk to it! I take a sugar cube, holding it with the tip of my thumb and index finger. I carefully bring it into delicate contact with the surface of the tea in my cup. I watch with glee the way the sugar sucks up the tea between my fingers; it changes from white to a light brown. The cube then dissolves, crumbling in my hand. I lick the remaining sweetness from my fingertips, even though my mother hates it when I do this. After a little while, David daintily removes a black raisin from his mouth and places it at the edge of his plate, apologizing, "Sorry, it's a fly that hasn't been boiled properly." They all laugh in the same way.

He then asks his usual question:

—When are you coming to visit us in Basra? I'll admit that it's hot and humid, but we have some new friends from Italy whom we'd like you to meet.

My mother answers him:

—My husband doesn't want me to leave here. He wants me to become accustomed to their lifestyle before I start moving around.

Millie says:

—Haven't you got used to it after all these years?

—I'm still trying, but he insists that I must stay with my daughter; I'm supposed to wait for her to come home from school every day. Even going to Baghdad for the day has become difficult because there's so little time.

David:

—Can't you leave her with her father for a weekend and give yourself a short break?

My mother says despairingly:

—He doesn't believe in that, and if I did, he'd leave her with those Gypsies all the time; I'm worried that she'll catch some awful disease from them.

Millie says with a smile:

—Oh, don't exaggerate; we've even stopped boiling the water before we drink it, the way we used to when we first came out here. It's merely a matter of time; you'll stop worrying about cleanliness, sterilization, and table manners, especially at mealtimes. Life here depends on the weather, and how hot it is. Heat doesn't obey any schedules.

—Yes, Millie, but my husband is so hot-tempered, we end up arguing all the time. You know I wanted to send her to England for her schooling, but since my parents died and their house in Ealing was sold, I have no one left to look after her in London. I spent most of what I had on my preparations to join my husband out here, and now there's nothing left for me to go back to. I can't even think of anyone I could visit at Christmastime.

Millie's tone becomes serious.

—You're tired. You were lonely back there, and now you're living alone in a foreign land. We wish you could join us.

Mother:

—I have no choice. You know the story. I thought . . . I thought that the countryside out here was the way he described it to me. The magical East, with a glorious sunrise and a romantic sunset, days flitting by in an indescribable purple haze of charm and fantasy. The reality turned out to be a stifling heat that climbs up the palm trees. Flies in the morning, mosquitoes in the evening, and the screeching of winged cockroaches that jump around in my bedroom at dawn! I'm sure that you, too, have spent many a hot evening when the electricity's been cut off, trying to trap them in the dark by the light of a candle or a lantern. And now I've got this terrible allergy every spring from the apricots. If I wanted to swim, the mud from the river would be toxic to my skin, and I'd probably get raped anyway. As for sunbathing—that is out of the question in an area like this.

David asks her with some optimism:

—Why don't you talk him into moving down to Basra? There are so many foreigners living in the area; all the services we need are provided for us. You would find nothing is missing.

—Oh, that's not possible. The lab and the flavorings factory that he has dealings with have both just been set up in this area. We'll have to stay here as long as he remains contracted to them. He's also very attached to this rural lifestyle, which reminds him of his youth. I can hardly believe this is the same man I met when he came to study in England.

Millie exchanged a quick glance with her brother.

—Our company is looking for foreign employees. We've submitted your details. Think about it. Discuss things with him. Things might change for some reason or another in the near future. The offer is valid for three months.

My mother sighs deeply, then continues in a low voice:

—Were it not for the girl, I'd do it.

David turns to me, saying with his usual smile:

—What about you, my little princess, when will you come to visit us with Mummy?

I answer:

—When my father comes.

Then I added:

—Dawood.

Father, you said you wouldn't be away for long, but I seem to see you only at the end of the week. You're busy with your work, while my mother is busy with her moisturizers, caring for her skin. The raised voices in the house have quieted down because you are never here. You don't plait my braid for me in the morning anymore; you don't whisper your instructions in my ear as you take me to school. Words that make me worry: "Don't spend too much time playing with the boys"; "Playing with marbles isn't for girls"; "Let the others ride the bicycles"; "I want you to excel in your studies this year." You have arranged for me to go to school in that big yellow bus. It makes me dizzy. The older children pinch me from behind the seats. They make fun of the darkness of my skin, saying, "Here comes the black girl!" My mother likes to sleep late. There's no need for me to wake her up to help me tie my shoelaces or to straighten my collar. My food has been prepared for me the night before, and if she were to wake up early with me, she'd simply warn me before I leave, "Don't talk to strangers!"

When I return in the afternoon, I find her sitting on the sofa. Her hair is rolled up in a white towel like a turban. She always wears it like that after she has a bath. She says that when it's hot, she spends her time reading what she calls "light" novels. She then exchanges them with David and Millie during their brief, infrequent visits. Her teeth are biting onto a plastic tube with a lit cigarette at its end. She keeps her lips splayed apart to avoid smearing the white cigarette holder with her lipstick. She chose it in white to match the white towel and the white bathroom slippers. She has spread parallel lines of colored cards in front of her. She's playing solitaire again. Some locals showed her how to predict her luck using the cards. The King is raised high in the air, the Jack tumbles onto the Queen, the Joker has been turned facedown under a small saucer. An upturned coffee cup sits in the saucer. For fortune-telling, they also taught her how to drink bitter Turkish coffee, turning the cup over to read the unknown in the pattern of the coffee grains.

We exchange a brief greeting without kisses. She asks me:

—Have you started your dance lessons?

I answer her as I bite into a carrot that I've taken out of my pocket. I wipe away the fluff clinging to it.

—Not yet.

She lifts up a row of cards and puts them aside.

—Why not?

I bite into the carrot with appetite.

—Because the teacher is pregnant, and—

She interrupts me:

—Don't talk while you eat.

I remember how she stopped me from eating rice with my fingers the way you do with such delight, insisting that I use a knife and fork. She taught me the proper way to eat soup. I didn't know that soup should be sipped from the side of the spoon and not from its front.

I tell her:

—They're doing some alterations in the dance studio; they haven't given us the sports kit yet.

I ask her:

—Where is Father?

She answers in her usual style,

—With his flavorings.

Before she has the chance to make any further comments, a green phone, decorated with golden plastic numbers, rings. It makes a whirring sound, as if it has night crickets trapped inside it. My mother chats away, "Oh hello, Millie, how are you?"

This is my chance to visit the forbidden parts of the farm. Your daily preoccupation with your work and her numerous distractions in the afternoon mean that I can slip away—an occurrence that has become less frequent as the list of forbidden activities has lengthened. She recited them to me recently; you supported her. I must not eat at Khaddouja's house. I must not go with Hatem or Ubaid to the remote parts of the farm. I must not join the other children when they catch tadpoles in the ditches. I must never go near the beer factory at all. It was only then that I realized that time had any value. I left the house quickly, singing a little rhyme to myself which Ubaid normally sings:

> "Oh mother of Hussein, sit up right,
> Sell those tomatoes for two fils, right."

We were warned hundreds of times not to play on the riverbank. It's there that I find Khaddouja. She has lifted up her light dishdasha, gathering it in her arms. She's looking down at her two bare feet as they sink into the soft mud. Little bubbles emerge around the sides of her legs, bursting silently when they come into contact with the edge of her dishdasha, which is dangling down at the back. A turbid, dirty froth is gathering at her feet. She turns toward me and calls out, inviting me to join her. I quickly kick off my shoes and socks, lifting up my skirt the way she has done. My feet sink into the cool wet sand. The yellow froth wraps itself around my ankles. I call to her:

—Look, Khaddouja, I'm wearing two soap bracelets around my ankles!

She responds to my excitement with a gentle smile. When we get used to the coolness of the water, we start playing our game. We balance ourselves on one foot, and use the other one to pick up little twigs or blades of grass floating in the water nearby. We use our toes with incredible dexterity. We pick up the weeds and pass them to each other using our toes, trying to keep our balance on the other foot. The one who loses her balance and wobbles is the one who has lost the game.

I see myself with her on that distant riverbank, so far away now. When I miss our forbidden place, I recall the mystical flow of my childhood with Khaddouja; it's as if I'm still standing on one leg.

Near that spot are some evil-looking dry weeds we called Chickeek—"the Thornies." They're a form of cactus, dark in color; their fruits are like small prickly hedgehogs, each the size of a pistachio nut. We pick them with great care, knowing that their jabs are very painful. We quickly throw them at each other; they cling to our clothes, to our hair, and to our socks. We return covered with them. We don't know how to get rid of them, so the other children help us; Hatem, Aswad ("the Black One"), who is nicknamed, the son of the mother of the black one, and little Ulaiwee. All pick the thorny beads out of our hair, singing meaningless songs they make up during the day: "Tot . . . Haya . . . Nasir . . . Daya . . . Shid il Kur . . . Alal . . . Zambur." We join the others who are retrieving jummar, the delicious pulp buried deep inside the trunk of a palm tree. Once it's extracted, it's carefully distributed to all who are there. I ate the fresh delicacy with my friends; this was one treat my mother never found out about.

We awaken from our delightful reveries only when we hear Delleh's voice calling us from a distance. Why is it that mothers always seem to shout from afar?

The magic of the river beckons to us. But they had frightened us with the story of the Siluwa monster, who rises from the water to swallow little children. I always imagined this mythical creature as having one huge breast in the middle of her chest. Khaddouja's family always told us that she would devour us, not nurse us. But in my nightmares she had no other features except that one breast. In spite of that, I still preferred her to Snow White. Khaddouja's senile grandfather made the situation worse by telling us about Abdul Shat—the river monster, a huge black giant who lived in the waters of the Tigris and protected its banks. He told us that if we stayed by the river's edge for too long, the sun would burn our faces; we'd become black, just like the monster. Those two terrifying tales were enough to keep us away from the river and its secrets; we found the alternative in the mud by the irrigation ditches, where we were at least protected by the apricot trees. Whenever I was tempted to wade barefoot in the shallow waters there with Khaddouja, I'd see my mother's face and hear her stern voice warning me, "Don't you dare!"

I was repeating a little rhyme to myself as I was heading home, "Little chickpea cold, Little raisin hot, When the evening comes, You'll be in the pot!" I was thinking, were it not for the springtime at the apricot farm, all my childhood days with Khaddouja would be the color of dust. Like the color of the sky when the sandstorms raged in the summer as I played with her during the holidays. When I recall those days, it's that hue that I remember. That was the color of the cloudy water in the river, the mud on both sides of the irrigation ditches, the huts with pieces of straw encrusted in their walls. The tennour—the mud oven outside them—also was the color of dust, as were the round discs of dried cow dung stacked up in rows outside the primitive houses. I recall the stink: a mixture of dung and animal feed that hit me in the face each time I walked past their huts.

In the corners of those homes are mounds of baskets strewn on top of each other. They're all made of dried yellow reeds woven together. Underfoot is a brown mat, made from palm fronds; another hangs on the wall. Large earthenware pots hold the brown flour that Delleh uses to make their bread. She bakes it in the tennour, retrieving the flat round freshly baked bread from inside it. These khubuz circles emerge covered with large brown bubbles, giving them a thin crispy crust. From the tennour, Delleh heads toward the hib—a large earthenware container, conical in shape, used to filter drinking water. There are beads of sweat on her brow from the heat of the clay oven. The hib has numerous fissures on its outer surface that head off in all directions. The moisture seeps out through its walls, evaporates, and cools the water within. Little beads collect on the surface, like the sweat on her forehead.

The dust particles are everywhere; they cover the women's black abayas, their veils, their furniture, their cows, even their faces. It seems this is the secret magic dust of their vitality. Khaddouja's family is always rushing to and fro, blending into the color of their background. Even their complexions are brown, like the mud around them. They're all part of the same brown family, a coloring they've inherited unfailingly for generations. How strange I feel when they welcome me as one of them: "Here comes the girl with the round face the color of baked bread!"

2

You've organized a dinner party at our house for the first time. It's to celebrate the opening of the flavorings factory. Father, never before had I seen you so excited. I could even detect a slight blush in your cheeks in spite of the duskiness of your skin. And never before had I seen my mother looking so elegant, with you following her, repeating your comments about how short her dress was. They say she's beautiful. I suppose they're dazzled by the whiteness of her skin. But I could place my finger on every part of her body where she has fine blood vessels, like thin red hairs that could be seen underneath her skin. They're there in her armpits, and scattered sparsely on the arch of her feet. They remind me of the little hairy roots that had sprouted from the chickpeas I'd laid on a bed of wet cotton in the jar on my bedroom windowsill. Things like that are not noticed at parties!

My mother rang David and Millie to invite them, saying:

—The invitation is for seven P.M.

You rang your friends at the factory:

—We'll expect you from seven o'clock onwards—take your time.

My mother complains about the eastern disregard for punctuality. You explain to her:

—This is the way the invitation should be. It would be improper for us to insist on them arriving at a specific time. We're not in England, my dear.

They all arrived between seven and eight, except the elderly family physician and his young fiancée. Dr. George had been called away to an emergency at one of the houses in the industrial district.

The living room has filled up. Six of your business friends and three of their wives are here. One of them left his second wife at home, according to what the others are saying. The women's laughter cuts through the clouds of smoke floating above their heads. I watch their movements from the top of the stairs, enjoying the chance to observe the gathering without being noticed. The women sit with one leg crossed over the other, the upper one swinging to and fro repetitively; the bottom one is fixed. A shoe's pointed heel pierces the carpet, and every now and then, a pistachio-nut shell or the ash from one of their cigarettes falls onto it. The men are standing. Each has one hand in his pocket, while the other holds up a glass that sways right and left; the ice cubes clink against each other, set in motion by the vigor of their conversation. Father, you circulate among your guests, serving them all. Everybody will be up till dawn, but you will not forget to plait my braid in the morning before sending me off to school. Tomorrow is the day I must return my school report, after you've signed it.

Millie. I try to observe her small ears from afar, but David keeps blocking my line of vision as his broad shoulders shift, causing his sister to disappear from my sight completely. The shiny shoes increasingly walk about; they almost reflect the guests' movement across the room. The silk dresses dance around, and images of faces intersect each other; some are wearing glasses, others are wearing lipstick. Their voices reach me, but I don't understand their words. Some of the men are talking about a project to dry out the citrus fruits grown in the area and use their essence in industrial flavors. Another group is admiring the large Mazgouf fish that was grilled on an open fire and is now laid out in the center of the table. Some of the women are chatting about Orosdi, the wonderful new department store that has opened in Baghdad. My mother is seated between David and Millie. They're talking about Basra and the oil company. I wait until they're all busy elsewhere to slip into the kitchen. I lift the lid of the pot filled with boiled cobs of corn, take two out and head off to the farm.

On my way there, I hum the tune of something I learned at school. When the refrain of a song is going around in my head, I can't control it. It goes round and round like a scratched record. I can't get rid of it until I learn a new song. "One, two, three Alabee . . . Samira daughter of Chalabee . . . sits with her golden hair selling chickpea, chickpea . . ." Halfway through my song, I hear the sound of a car approaching our house. It must be the doctor and his young fiancée arriving.

Khaddouja was hovering outside her family's three huts, waiting to see what I would bring her from our party. She jumped up and down as I approached, eagerly taking the boiled cob of corn I'd brought her. We sat down on the colored mat in their hut. Her family had just vacated the spot, leaving behind a few morsels of their dinner. The mankala—a rectangular metal container filled with coal where they brew their tea—is still warm, with the empty teapot still lodged amid the white ashes. Beside it is a tray with a few glass beakers lying on their side. They contain a sugary liquid that has oozed out, and a few wet tea leaves still cling to their insides. On the outside of the glasses are some dark black fingerprints, stains from the charcoal. The sugar bowl has a block of mud stuck to its undersurface to weigh it down. Khaddouja told me that the man who repairs broken china was a relative of theirs; she showed me how he had repaired their cracked teapot.

Amma Zakiya, Khaddouja's eldest paternal aunt, came in. She's called Amma Keeka because of her famous short bursts of laughter: Kee-ka, kee-ka! She took away the empty tray, so we turned our attention to devouring the corncobs. I watched the rapturous way Khaddouja contemplated this novel item of food as she held it in her hands. With her index finger, she gently palpates the neat row of yellow beads. She turns it around, examining it from every angle. She licks the dissolved salt from its edges, then sucks the cob from both ends. She puts her tongue out; with its pointed tip, she feels the little dimple in the middle of each of the kernels. She finally starts to eat it, making chewing and sucking noises. If I did that in my mother's presence, she'd send me away from the dinner table with disgust: "Go up to your room without any supper!"

We hear the sound of a baby crying from the window of the room Zakiya has gone into. The wife of Khaddouja's youngest uncle on her mother's side has had another baby, who has been called Hadiya—"Gift from God." The baby carries on crying; we are drawn toward the open window. At that moment, Amma Keeka draws the cloth hanging from the nails on the inside of the window to hide Hadiya and her mother from any inquisitive eyes. But Khaddouja was determined to be there when the baby was to be breast-fed. She tells me, "Come and see the new baby." We enter the room. Both the women are too busy with other things; neither objects to our presence. We sit down in a corner observing the scene. The little baby is in a cradle surrounded by stained metal rails. Above it is a blue plastic flower with seven perforations. This is a talisman called Mother of Seven Eyes; it's meant to protect the baby from all harms and evil. The mother lifts up the covers, revealing the tiny creature, and removes a silk cloth that was once the quilt her mother used on her wedding day. It's now worn and threadbare, having finally become a bedcloth for Hadiya.

The mother holds her daughter in her arms. She takes her swollen breast out from underneath her dishdasha and lays it on the baby's face. The little one reaches out and grasps the nipple with her lips. She sucks her mother's milk with all her strength, exhausted by her hunger. A fly lands at the corner of her little mouth; another hovers around the purple nipple. Nobody pays any attention to the flies here—unlike my mother, if I've forgotten to shut the screen door behind me when I return home. The atmosphere has calmed down now that the baby is breathing more quietly. I ask Khaddouja about the bracelets the little one is wearing. Her two wrists, which look like two soft bars of dough, are encircled by neatly strung rows of black and white beads. The black and white beads alternate with no error whatsoever.

Khaddouja says:

—It's the bracelet for flesh and fat.

—Why is she wearing it?

—So that she grows bigger and stronger.

—Then why don't you wear one, Khaddouja, so that you too could become big and strong?

After a while I added:

—If you wore it long enough, you might become as big as the Siluwa monster!

Her two eyebrows came together in a stern frown in the middle of her dark face.

—Who told you I wanted to become a Siluwa?

—So what is it that you want, then?

—I want to go to school.

—But here it is much nicer than it is at school!

She objects, saying:

—But you have learned how to read and write. All I do is gather grass for the cows and bake bread for my mother.

—I'll teach you how to read, on one condition—

She interrupts me:

—But I have no shoes.

I tell her:

—I'll give you a pair of mine, on one condition.

—What is it?

—You teach me how to ride Hatem's bicycle and how to catch butterflies.

—Riding the bicycle is easy—catching butterflies is even easier.

She jumps up as she says that, throwing herself onto me, kissing me, and clapping her hands, adding:

—Welcome, welcome the blessing of God.

When Amma Zakiya feels that I've stayed with them for too long, she takes it upon herself to return me home to my parents. How I love those moments when she lifts me up with a quick graceful movement and sits me on her shoulder. One of my feet dangles down the front of her chest and the other lies over her shoulder blade. It is the traditional way that the people of Zafraniya carry their children, something I never encountered again elsewhere. I lay my hands on the futa covering her. I feel like the pots of yoghurt she carries one on top of the other on her head as she walks along the farm tracks, perfectly balanced, her wide abaya flapping in the breeze with a rural elegance, colored by the dust.

On our way home, about halfway there, we go past an unused stable. A naked lightbulb hangs just outside it, dangling down like a glowing onion, with swarms of mosquitoes circling around it. I watch the little insects competing with each other, producing a low, unpleasant buzzing. They fight for a lick of the pale illumination no larger than a football in the middle of the surrounding darkness. Zakiya bends down, saying, "Mind your head!" Whenever we go past that spot, she's concerned that the electric current flowing through the drooping wires might injure me. We're finally there, and she hands me over to the night watchman.

A brief moment later I find myself in my bed. A thin ribbon of light filters into my room from beneath the door. Through the keyhole, a finger of smoke carries up the sound of the women downstairs, laughing among themselves.

A new ditty that I pick up at school the next day from a younger girl is going around in my head. I heard it on my way home and kept singing it as the yellow bus did its rounds. "Kash, Keesh, Saffaron, Miss Zubeida is a Mrs." I found myself still singing it as I came through the front door. I've passed my exams this semester, but I can't recall how that happened. We learn our lessons by heart, but all that remains in my head are those catchy rhymes. I hate math lessons and everything to do with numbers. When Miss Juliette comes into the classroom and starts going through the multiplication tables, I start whispering to myself, "Little fart, smelly fart, Farted by the Effendi, my educated Turkish Lord."

School was just an unending daze of songs, ugly teachers, and boring numbers. The loneliness of my first day there taught me about the differences in sizes. I came to the conclusion that my childhood had ended when the little coffee table I once leaned against to stand up and walk had become small enough for me to knock over with a kick. I later learned that this game of sizes was also very important during dance lessons. I open the front door, "Kash, Keesh . . ." I hear your voice, Father, from the kitchen. Your conversation is in a dry English:

—I've already told you, no means no!

I hear my mother's high-pitched voice:

—It's an opportunity I can't afford to miss, especially now that the company has opened an office in Baghdad!

You answer her in a tone I would have been able to recognize even if your argument had been taking place in the middle of the farm,

—You don't need to work! I'm working very hard on this project and will provide all you need in the house. It's just a question of time!

—Yes, dear . . .

She never calls you "dear"; she uses that word only when she's very upset. She carries on:

—It's indeed a question of time. How long am I going to remain in this primitive, isolated place, doing nothing and not speaking your language?

You answer:

—Until the girl is old enough to look after herself. Raising a daughter is more difficult in this part of the world than raising a son. We don't neglect them when they are little. I'm sure you must have learned that in the time that you've been here!

Slowly and stealthily I creep toward the kitchen door. I can hear her saying:

—The girl, the girl! How long are you going to keep using her as an excuse? I need a change, and the company needs a secretary! I can type—why are you stopping me?

—Woman, try to understand my situation. Yesterday I allowed you to drink openly, and I pretended not to notice the soft way you danced with Dawood in front of my friends and their wives. I make no objections when you want to mix with your friends. I'll see how long you'll keep using Millie as an excuse! But I will not allow you to work outside the house. You don't need to do that, and certainly not while the girl is still in primary school.

—You comment about my drinking and my dancing as though you were doing me a favor. What about your friends, who have a wife for parties and another one for the home?

—We disagree for the millionth time. Let's stop criticizing our traditions and comparing them to what you consider civilized. I'm asking you to forget everything else and concentrate on this: contradictions don't matter; all I want for my daughter is that you persevere with us until she has grown up. Is that understood?

Suddenly, I hear a little hiccup from her; the argument has quieted down. I don't know what to do. I'd never seen her cry, but that was undoubtedly what I was hearing through the kitchen door. Maybe her tears are white, like the color of her skin. I feel nothing! You've noticed the edge of my skirt and you get up to greet me. You denied me my one chance of seeing her cry. With a rapid gesture, you shut the door, leaving her inside, and take me up the stairs to your bedroom.

I can't keep up with you as you go up the stairs to your room at the far end of the corridor on the upper floor. Your long strides take you up the steps like a dusky colored stork. Your bed is on the right side of the room by the wall. Beside it is a little television, which sits on a square table. There is a piece of cardboard paper folded up several times and wedged under one of its legs to stop it from rocking. The set is always left on. The two-seater sofa underneath the window faces the door. In front of it is a low coffee table covered with newspapers, press clippings, and business correspondence. Everything is piled up on top of everything else. I see piles of documents on the table—*The Gazette of Iraqi Law*, a book about food and nutrition, and articles about solar energy. The two other walls in your room are filled with shelves and more shelves, which hold the largest collection of boxes I've ever seen in my life.

There are containers the size of a finger, others as big as a chair. There are strange cardboard boxes with unusual

names. Exotic fragrances waft out of them; I can almost lick
their taste from the air. There are metal cylinders with the
word THICKENERS written on them. Silver foil bags stapled
at the side, with red warning stickers—KEEP AWAY FROM
DIRECT SUNLIGHT; NATURAL STABILIZERS. Dark-colored
plastic gourds that resemble bottles of liquid medicine,
with large warnings in bold lettering: AVOID EXCESSIVE
HUMIDITY. On a carton lying next to them are the words
GUM ARABIC. There are transparent nylon sacks, their
necks sealed with rubber bands. Their contents are an unbelievable array of colors and hues.

On one of the upper shelves is a long row of test tubes,
six centimeters long, containing the most beautiful sugary
powders. The rays of sunlight pass through the glass tubes
left by the window, making their contents look like crystals partially dissolved in a dilute solution of blue clouds
and cotton. They're like a rainbow of timid turquoise that
has been captured and imprisoned in those slim tubes. A
small hole in one of the brown paper bags releases a green-
ish powder, just like the grains of sand passing through the
waist of an hourglass. A small mound the size of a hazelnut
has accumulated on the shelf in front of me. When you turn
on the fan, a little dust cloud is released from the green
hazelnut. It makes me sneeze. I say:

—What is this? Shouldn't we put it into an unbroken
bag?

You slow down the electric fan. For some strange reason,
the fan in your room works the opposite way from all the
other fans in the house. It spins at its top speed when it is
set on 1, it slows down when it is set on 2, and slows down
even further when it is set on 3. You say:

—It's the electrician's fault. No, there's no need for another bag, I'm going to get rid of it. This is a mixture for cake with lime flavor. It didn't work in the trial, so we're going to drop it from the project.

The word "project" remained associated in my mind with the rhyme "Kash, Keesh . . ." and the smell of carrot halawa dessert, both spinning around in my head. I tried to make a connection between my mother crying in the kitchen and the new terms you wanted me to learn about something called an acid and something else called an alkali. This sweet dust will turn into honey in my lungs if I breathe it in deeply. Yesterday, I finished reading my storybook about Alice in Wonderland. I had read it in my mother's English; but the white rabbit belonged here. I could visualize him hiding behind those shelves, looking at his pocket watch, late and in a hurry, jumping over the papers, bags, and boxes. He picks the magic colors, flavorings, and fragrances to paint the route that Alice might walk along in her next dream!

You ask me:

—You passed your exams, didn't you?

—Yes, don't you remember signing my report card?

You reply, appearing distracted and distant:

—Yes, that's right, my clever little one.

You sit me down on the sofa beside you. You hold my hand and tell me in that tone of voice that I usually find frightening:

—I want you to listen to me well, my daughter. You're growing up, and you've started to understand. I want you to pass your exams every year. I want to be happy when I sign your report card. Don't preoccupy yourself with anything other than your studies and doing your homework. The most important thing for you is to get the top grades in your class.

—I can't get the top grades in my class. My mother doesn't help me with my homework because she doesn't understand Arabic. All my friends who get top grades get help from their mothers at home.

—I'll help you with your homework, then.

—When? You aren't here when I get back, and when you do get back, I'm fast asleep.

—On Fridays, then.

—Fridays! What about Khaddouja? When will I get to see her? I've promised her that I'd teach her how to read.

You rub your forehead for a brief moment using two fingers, then suddenly you've found the solution.

—All right, then, you don't have to get the top grades, but you must pass your exams every year.

We'd agreed.

I had saved up my next question from when we were coming up the stairs.

—Baba, why is my mother crying?

You get up from the sofa and switch off the television:

—She isn't crying!

—But I heard her, and I heard you arguing. She wants to work with Millie and you won't let her.

—Your mother wants to work because she's bored and she doesn't like the farm. It's very hot for her out here— she's not used to these temperatures. Her friend Millie is cleverer than she is. Your mother can't be like her. Your mother's place is here with me, with us. Don't worry.

—But she will leave us, I heard her on the phone the other day saying that she will leave this place someday.

You answer with irritation:

—Where would she go?

You then add:

—She has no one.

—She might take me with her.

You interrupt me, clearly upset:

—That is impossible, you're not going anywhere!

You then add:

—You're staying here on the farm. How could you leave your friends from the riverbank?

—But how could she leave on her own?

—Let's stop talking about this. Nobody is leaving here, I want you to understand that. It's true that we don't agree about everything in the house—she has her ways and I have mine, but that doesn't change things. She'll still be here waiting for you when you come home from school, you'll keep passing your exams every year, and I'll be at my job every day. Everybody is staying where they are!

You leave the room, but on the way out, you turn and say:

—That's a promise!

That night I dreamt I heard the engine of Dawood's car pulling up outside our house and the front door slamming shut loudly. I went down the stairs to the kitchen in the morning and said, "Good morning, Mummy." She turned around; it was Millie! Her small mouth had no teeth and was drawn inward. Her delicate lips were painted with a dark brown lipstick; she always followed the latest fashions. She said with no hesitation as she took a step toward me, "I'll be looking after you from now on." Her brown gummy mouth, which was puckered inward, looked like a contracting star underneath her nostrils. It reminded me of the thin stray dog's bottom as he wandered aimlessly on the farm nearby. I took a big step backward; the scene changed into a cloud. I woke up a few minutes later in my own bed, terrified at dawn.

What you told me turned out to be true. Nobody has gone away. My mother still waits for me when I come home from school; I pass my exams every semester; and you spend the whole day at work. As for Khaddouja, she taught me how to ride Hatem's bicycle in return for the first four letters of the alphabet, Alif, Ba, Ta, Tha. She couldn't learn the others; nor was she able to write them. She found it very difficult to hold the pencil properly. But she still taught me how to catch butterflies. She uses her dishdasha and pounces on them. I do my best to catch them with my skirt. After that, I decided to offer her a new game. One afternoon, I headed toward their huts to tell her about it. I found Hijjia Fanous—"Lantern"—cleaning the main room.

I go in looking for Khaddouja. Hijjia Fanous is very fat. I watch her moving slowly around the room. I smile as I remember how we followed her one evening as she headed to the spot they use to relieve themselves. We spied on her, watching her lift up her thick dishdasha and squat down. We were amazed by the number of blue tattoos she has on her buttocks, which resemble a giant apple, mounted onto two enormous thighs. She has intricate designs and Bedouin patterns on every bit of her skin; it's like a moving embroidered carpet. I exchanged glances with Khaddouja at that moment and we both burst out laughing. We were near enough for her to hear us and she turned around and shouted at us angrily. She bent over and picked up a small pebble, which she threw in our direction, but it missed us. Now I ask her:

—Hijjia Fanous, where's Khaddouja?

She answers dryly:

—I don't know.

—Hijjia, why are you destroying the spiders' homes?

She answers curtly,

—These webs are the devil's nasal slime. They bring us evil and must be cleared away!

Khaddouja comes in and interrupts the fun I'm having teasing Hijjia Fanous. I leave her to her demons and turn to my friend, to show her the new game. It involves a small wire that is twisted into the shape of a circle with a handle. I dip the metal ring into a bowl of soapy water. A shining layer of the liquid clings to it, creating a slippery film that covers the whole of the ring. I bring it closer to my mouth, purse my lips, and blow gently into it. A fragile bubble starts to grow on the other side. Khaddouja cries out "Allah" in amazement as she watches me blowing more bubbles. It's her turn next; she's thrilled by the way she can control the size of the transparent spheres. We dance amid the soap bubbles that are floating in the air; their surface glistens with quivering little colored windows. Shades of purple, pink, and blue are reflected in the sunlight. They burst on our clothes and on our hair, releasing a magical smell. I say to her:

—We learned this game at school, Khaddouja.

She twirls amid the bubbles. They disperse from in front of her; others burst on the tip of her nose. She says:

—You're so lucky, I wish I went to school.

But she didn't. She joined all the others who didn't leave here for a long time. It was as though you, Father, had predicted everyone's fate. Khaddouja remained where she was.

She spent her mornings with her mother. They washed clothes, gathered grasses for the cows, carried in the jugs of milk, and collected dried twigs. She added her contribution to the pile of wood stored outside their huts. She would come across Ubaid hiding behind a wall. He has stolen some tobacco and has rolled it up in a square white sheet of paper. He licks it and lights its tip. She threatens him, "Just you wait, I'll tell my uncle." He puts out his tongue and furrows his brow to frighten her. She leaves him alone and runs off to chase a fresh grasshopper. It leads her toward the beehives. She remembers the nasty sting she got from one of the honeybees last Friday and heads back toward the cows.

I once asked her:

—Why does your cow have a swollen bag underneath her stomach with so many fingers hanging down from it?

She replies without even looking at me:

—So that we have enough milk and don't go hungry.

—Yesterday I saw the chicks drinking from the cow's fingers.

She turned around and looked at me in disbelief:

—That can't be, chicks don't suckle.

—They do, I saw them.

She replied sharply:

—Don't lie! The chicks can't reach the cow's udder!

So my wild childhood friend put an end to my visions of moving images, which I exchanged with my mother. She used to tell me at bedtime, "Close your eyes and imagine a flock of sheep moving about in front of you. Try to count them—you'll find yourself drifting away into a relaxed sleep."

I found it impossible to explain to Khaddouja the idea of the moving flock of sheep, or the thought of the suckling chickens. I also found out that what made me laugh meant nothing to her, and what hurt her was alien to me. When their cow Najma—"star"—died, the whole family grieved for it. I felt sorry that they had lost one of their miserable animals, but I couldn't understand how a cow could mean so much to them. I told her the first joke I'd learned in my life.

—Khaddouja, I've got a joke to tell you.

She sat up and listened.

—Tell me.

—Two tomatoes were crossing the road. The first one got to the other side safely. She turned around and realized that her friend had been run over by a car. She sighed a little and then said to the squashed tomato, Come on, Ketchup!

She didn't laugh! It was only then I realized that things had started to change.

We spent six years at the farm. I can hardly believe that your determination not to leave kept us there for so long. I don't know how my mother coped with the heat; each summer was worse than the one that had gone before. She started to amuse herself by making alterations in the house. She began by repainting all the walls on the upstairs floor. After a while she decided to redecorate all the walls on the ground floor with different designs and patterns. She then declared war on the termites that were boring their way through the garden wall. She would disappear into the garden shed and rummage through the shelves laden with boxes that rattle, returning with some pink tablets called

Fattak—"exterminator." They look like grains of wheat and are treated with poisons and bitter toxins to kill off the rats. She examines a metal can filled with insecticide; its label reads Tarrad—"Chaser." And that's what I call one of the boys who runs after half the girls at school.

She draws up kerosene into plastic medical syringes, injecting it into the termites' raised burrows, which have popped up here and there. She takes off her rubber gloves, leaving them by the gas canisters that stand outside the kitchens in all the homes. They look like short, stout dwarfs; the protective metal rings around their spouts are all dented as a result of repeated use. We always had mouse-traps in the storeroom. Its other contents varied with the seasons. There was the season of washing the curtains, a season to lay out the carpets, and the season to roll them all away again when the winter was over. Throughout the cold season the Aladdin heating stoves were filled with kero-sene by the vendor with his blackened hands. He would help bring them in through the back door.

With the arrival of the summer season, the air coolers had to be cleaned using soft straw and pure water. It was the time when David and Millie came to give my mother a hand. I used to watch them every year from my bedroom window. When they'd finished cleaning all the air coolers, they started spraying each other with the cool water from the green rubber hose that danced like a snake under their bare feet. My mother wouldn't let me join them.

The new season has started. The school bus drops me off outside the house and speeds away in a cloud of dust. I walk down the narrow garden path leading to the storeroom, but there's no sign of the green garden hose or my mother's friends. After a little while I hear the sound of English laughter emerging from a small gap in the wall of the garden store. The door is shut, I dare not intrude. I approach a small opening in the leaking wall where the moisture has eaten away its edges and peer into the storeroom. A vertical pillar obstructs my view; all I can see is the opposite wall. I glance to the right and to the left, attempting to lick with my eyes each and every corner. I try to catch a glimpse of the source of the laughter. I listen. The intermittent chuckles come from behind the pillar, interspersed with other strange sounds.

The sunlight penetrates a small window high up on the eastern wall of the shed; its rays descend on what is hidden from my view behind the pillar, casting shadows onto the facing wall. I see the reflection of a canister of gas, the broken rocking chair, and the tool chest. Suddenly I see shadows with rounded corners. I see the shadow of two broad shoulders towering above the shadow of hair coiled up in a bun. Where is Millie? The shadows mingle, the bun tumbles and the hair hangs down. The envelopment increases. The rocking chair is set into motion. They are sharing it. The wall in front of me is a scene of colliding shadows. The moist peephole is tight around my eye. Millie is not there. The broken chair is rocking, rocking, rocking. I put my thickest two fingers in my ears and tear my eyes away from the moist fish mouth. I run.

For six years my mother has been fighting time with all kinds of activities. She has become obsessed with changing the furniture. She exchanges the old furniture with expensive, often imported pieces; yet you never object. One day she wanted to throw out all the kitchen furniture and replace it with modern fitted cupboards. All you said to her was, "Why not?" Quite frequently, I'd come home to find something new in the house. Another item would appear, and another corner of the house would be changed. Soon, all the empty space was taken up, except in your room, where the mounds of powders and boxes of flavors multiplied, and the floor was covered with magazines and lab reports; nothing here was changed.

When David suggested indoor plants to my mother, she took up the hobby. Branches hung down from the ceiling. They flourished throughout the house. Every corner had a seasonal plant: a cactus, a creeper, or a climber. It seemed that my bed was the only place where she didn't sow any seeds!

THE SILENCE IS SO UNUSUAL. I'm not used to hearing hushed voices in our house. Maybe the plants absorb the sounds. Your work commitments have increased. You disappear in your new car on Saturday mornings, the first day of the working week. I wave to you from the yellow school bus heading toward the city, while you drive down the little road through the fields leading to your project site. We don't meet till Thursday evening, the beginning of the weekend. My mother isn't bothered if I slip away stealthily to spend an afternoon or two with Khaddouja while she sleeps. My mother doesn't seem to care about a lot of things nowadays, especially the minor details that used to upset her so much in the past. As she moves around the house, it seems to me that she is gliding over a small cloud that separates her feet from the ground she treads upon. It's as though she has lost the ability to walk like the rest of us. She makes no sound when she moves, like footsteps on a cushion of air. I look at her. I see her face in one place and her thoughts in another, as if she's forgotten them in the next room. It has become difficult to discern more than two separate emotions in her face in an entire day. Throughout the afternoon, she would frequently gaze at the reflection of her face in the mirror— as she climbs the stairs, or as she enters the bathroom.

My mother no longer insists that I learn her English. She's now able to use some Arabic phrases. She surprised us when I came home with the invitation card for the parents' meeting at my school. You were planning on going, but she put her hand on her hips and said, "Should it not be me, her mother, who attends this meeting?" We chuckled at the way she'd expressed herself in broken Arabic, and that lightened the gloom of the previous days. In any case, her distracted state of mind didn't last for long. There was a phone call from the lab on a Wednesday evening; they asked her to go there straightaway. An ambulance had been called to take you to the hospital a few minutes before they'd rung her. A cloud of worry gathered on her forehead. I'd never seen her concentrate so hard. She grabbed her handbag and headed for the door. I could hear the sound of her high heels clicking as she headed out. That thin layer of cushioning had disappeared. She said without turning around, "Wait by the phone!" Then she went out.

You were away from us for two whole weeks, during which time I didn't go out to see Khaddouja. The day after the phone call, I'd told her, "My father is ill." Delleh, who was standing next to her, replied, "We will pray that he regains his health, and that he will be up on his feet again very soon." She then took her daughter by the hand and led her away. Two days later we received a jug of fresh milk from their new cow. They had called it Nejima—"Little star." I waited for you. I couldn't go into your room. The key was in your pocket the day you were taken ill at the lab. I would stop and smell the flavorings through the keyhole, and then continue on my way up or down. You eventually came home to us when elderly Dr. George, who had been treating you, allowed you out of hospital. He accompanied you home, without his fiancée this time. You welcomed him to our house, "Please come in, Abu Salah, come in," using the traditional Arab way of greeting him, calling him Father of Salah, the name of his firstborn son. I was shocked by the pallor of your smile. My mother had prepared a bed for you on the ground floor. The instructions were that there should be minimal exertions for another two weeks. The doctor is saying to you, "Don't forget, a heart attack is not a minor thing." My mother is talking to the elderly man in the corridor, speaking to him rapidly in English. He answers her with no hesitation; they understand each other without the need for any hand gestures. Very quietly I slip over to where you are lying. I find it so strange that I can't smell the fragrance of fruits on your clothes. I sit on your bed close to your face. A little tear trembles in the angle of your right eye.

A few days later my mother announces that she's going to learn how to drive. For the first time, you don't argue! And for the first time, I've discovered that I can think! I learned how to think slowly, the way my mother was learning to drive a car. I started thinking in my room, at school, and even on the farm.

It's Friday. I venture out after breakfast with my latest

discovery. I feel that my every step now has a new presence; I can think. On my way to the river, I see the only person who wears colored rubber slippers. They aren't gray or black like the ones worn by all the men and women who live in the mud huts. She's a woman they call Aunt Rikin—"Corner." It's a distinctive name, like her unusual red rubber slippers. She's standing outside the hut on the right, making a fan out of colored palm fronds. She makes a large number of them every month and sells them when the hot summer season arrives. Aunt Rikin, also known as Um al Mihafeef—the fan seller—walks past me. Her mounds of flesh move under her tight dishdasha, making a scratching sound as the material rubs against her skin. Her rubber slippers also make a funny hissing noise, fssst, fssst. She's just washed her feet and the rubber slippers' pores have become saturated with water. On her left cheek is an irregular brown scar that has eroded part of her nostril. They call it a "Baghdad boil" and it eats away the skin it has affected. I never saw her do anything all year other than weave fans for the summer season.

She has a sister called Sa'adiya—"the happy one." I very rarely notice her among the others. She hides away from people, waiting to get married. Her face is covered with greasy red spots, and there are places on her cheeks where the skin has peeled off, revealing the yellowed encrustations underneath. I find her appearance a little frightening. I came across her that day sitting underneath the lonely touckee-berry tree at the edge of the farm. She's gathering the fruit that has fallen around the massive tree trunk. Some of the berries are still whole; the others have become dark stains, like red spit, on the ground where she's been sitting. Sa'adiya carries on what she's doing. She picks up the berries that have fallen near to her, crushes them with her hand, and lifts the fruity flesh to her face. She's wiping her cheeks with the red juice, hoping that it will heal the red spots and cure her. Both Delleh and Bibi Hijjia told her that her spots would settle only when she got married. And so she's still waiting with hope. I felt sorry for her. I offered her a sugar cube, like the ones my mother offers her friends when they come around for tea. Sa'adiya had never in her life seen sugar in the form of cubes, but she still declined what I was offering. I felt hurt and walked away. The pang I carried inside was the size of that sugar cube—it soon melted, the way the sugar cube melted in my hand. Little did I know of the catastrophe that was looming on the horizon.

The next few days passed unbelievably slowly. Movements around the house were dictated by instructions from the hospital, the thermometer, the sphygmomanometer, and visits from Abu Salah. You were eventually allowed to go back to the project, but only twice a week. You begged to be allowed to do more. He told you, the way doctors do:

—Overworking would be very bad for you. You could collapse again. Please look after yourself. I'm asking you this as a friend.

—But Doctor, my work is so important to me, and the project is being expanded.

—We all have important things to do. I know that you've achieved excellent results in the past few years. It's time to count your blessings.

—I'll die if I'm unable to do my work, you know that.

—I know that my dear friend, but you'll kill yourself if

you keep working this hard. Try to find yourself an amusing hobby. Read something during this period of enforced rest while your heart is regaining its strength.

The doctor picked up his black bag and disappeared through the front door. You covered your face with the white bed sheet, and you too disappeared.

We have a new item of furniture in the house. My mother wants to know what I think of it. It's a very large piece sitting in the living room. It has been placed in the corner facing your bed. My mother removes the covers. A smile lights up your face. A piano! Is this for me? What am I going to do with all these black and white keys? I sit on the chair and caress the shiny polished wood. I run my fingers over the keys without striking them. Their infinite number frightens me. I look into your eyes, and I realize what your new interest is going to be. My mother is saying:

—You'll have a piano teacher who will come here to give you lessons starting next week.

She then adds,

—Your father insists that you learn your lessons and train at home every afternoon.

I repeat after her like an echo:

—Every afternoon!

She answers:

—Yes.

I understood what that meant; no argument.

I thought to myself, For the time being at least.

It was in this way that a new reality came into my life—music. I found great difficulty in concentrating on what Mr. Jalal was saying in the house, after being used to spending the afternoon gliding among the apricot trees. I spent hours with him every week. Sometimes I'd look forward to his visits with anticipation; at other times I'd find the endless repetition of set tunes monotonous. Sometimes I'd totally reject his strict instructions, especially if he'd just eaten a meal prepared with generous amounts of garlic, which was the way his wife seemed to cook most of their meals. During the first week, classes started just after lunchtime; he taught me all about notes and octaves as he breathed out those unpleasant odors. Starting then I imagined that the sol-fa musical scales would always smell of garlic!

I couldn't convince you, Father, to limit his visits to just twice a week. Then one evening I heard loud knocking on our front door. I stopped playing do, re, mi and listened. The knocking became louder. No one went to open the door. I left my music teacher and went to see who it might be. It was Hatem, out of breath and overcome with emotion, spitting out his words:

—For God's sake, come quickly!

I felt a strange fear, something I'd never experienced before in my childhood.

—What's wrong, Hatem?

He didn't answer me. He just turned around and started running, so I followed him. We headed down the path between the apricot trees, racing with each other. I heard my mother calling out to me to come back at once. The sound of her voice was muffled by the clouds of dust raised by our pounding feet.

When we reached the three huts by the riverside, we found half of the family lingering outside. The rest had gathered in the middle hut. As I entered through the door, I could hear the sound of loud screams shaking the mud walls. The women were crying without pausing to draw breath; among them I could hear Delleh's voice, which I'd been unable to hear initially. I'd never seen any of them crying before. It had never occurred to me that these people cried! My heart trembled when I heard those sounds. I imagined that I could hear the notes do, fa, and sol in their wailing. I could feel my legs giving way with terror as I approached Delleh. Her dusty dry face was moistened with tears. The men were chanting, "There's no god but Allah"; the children were hiding behind the dishdashas of the grown-ups. Their faces appeared puzzled. Should they cry with the others, or not? I couldn't understand what was happening. No one would explain to me what catastrophe had befallen Delleh. She lifted her swollen eyes up and glanced in my direction. The whites looked boiled in hot tears. She wailed, "My daughter is gone . . . I've lost my little one . . ."

My joints felt weak as I understood what had happened. That white bundle laid out on the floor by her mother was Khaddouja. All I remember after that was someone's hand pulling me away from that awful sight.

Death and Khaddouja . . . I was unable to link the two!

They told me that she'd come down with bilharziasis. They explained to me that her lifeblood had drained away every time she urinated into the irrigation ditches, and that the continuing blood loss had ended her life. My mother rushed me to the doctor even though you had told her in a condescending tone that it was not possible for me to acquire the disease through human contact. The only way I could catch Khaddouja's illness was by doing what she had done—wading in stagnant water. Her father, Kadhim, told me that her soul had gone up to God. My mother said she'd become an angel and now danced in the sky. I spent many days willing her to return, but she didn't.

Dr. George came to visit us again. I heard him talking to my mother behind closed doors. He mentioned depression and how we all needed a change of scenery. It seemed that the time for our move to the city had come. My mother's dream had finally become the best solution for us. She started to pack in preparation for our move to Baghdad. This time, you didn't object. Khaddouja's death and the deterioration of your health had changed me into a different girl.

My final recollections of Zafraniya are of that last Friday before we left the farm for good. The afternoon started with the sound of an engine that all the children in that area knew well. I stayed with them at the end of the road, awaiting the arrival of the large truck that came to those parts every other season. One group of children shouted with glee, "The smoke truck is coming!" Another group got ready to run; I could hear the pounding of dozens of little feet. Among them is Gazala—deer—Khaddouja's little cousin. They run behind the truck that is spewing thick smoke behind it as it makes its way through the orchards and the tree groves to spray them with pesticide, killing all the insects. We were told this was done to preserve the crops. We paid no attention to what was said about how it killed the mosquitoes. We ran along inside that thick white chemical cloud in spite of the pungent smell, until we were overcome with our coughing and choking and tears flowed from our reddened eyes. The fat driver stuck his head out of the window, shouting at us:

—This smoke will kill you just like it kills the bugs!

We carry on doggedly for a few stolen moments of dizziness and the thrill of disappearing in that thick white cloud. The driver speeds off, and we all get left behind at varying distances. We wipe our eyes and dust down our clothes. We are spread out along the road: different heights, different sizes. That day I noticed that I was the tallest girl in the group. In the distance I could hear the sound of the pumping station, taking the water from the river and sending it down the irrigation ditches to a nearby farm. Dub, dub, dub.

3

Our new home is in Rasafa, that area of Baghdad built on the eastern side of the Tigris. It's situated at the entrance of the seventh street branching off from Attar Road, heading in the direction of the Abu Klam petrol station. We share our garden wall on the eastern side of the house with a Jewish family. Beyond their house is the Orthopedic Hospital. I don't know why I always called it the new home when in fact it was a fairly old house. We had to repair it, redecorate it, and treat the termite colonies that had left their trails all over. A nabuk—lotus jujube tree—stands elegantly in the center of the garden; at the far end is a young palm tree, barely as high as the wall that separates our house from the road. David and Millie helped us move our belongings. You're not allowed to exert yourself.

The rhythm of our lifestyle hasn't changed very much from the time when we were living in the Expert's House. You plait my braid for me before the school bus arrives. My mother eats an English pancake with lemon juice and sugar. You have the local Alban dairy cream with honey. She washes her face using a soft wet cloth, without soap, to avoid damaging her complexion. You blow your nose into your handkerchief—khh, khh, khh. You still prefer the mid-

69

day meal, ending it by dipping your bread lovingly into a saucer of some 'AA' brand date syrup mixed with a generous helping of sesame-seed oil. Whereas she never misses what she calls "afternoon tea" and her favorite sandwiches of jam and butter.

You carry on the same never-ending rituals—you light a stick of incense every Friday, while she lights a candle every Sunday. She smokes before breakfast, only brushing her teeth afterward. You prefer to use chewing gum, or you clean between your teeth using a matchstick that you've peeled using your fingernails. I collect the nabuk fruits in my dishdasha. I then sit and eat them alone under the tree. My mother says that the smell of the little fruits reminds her of children's vomit, especially if I've put them in a nylon bag and forgotten them in the kitchen. The tree's end came when my mother decided that it was dropping too many leaves, creating unnecessary rubbish in the garden. The time had come for it to be cut down and its remains burned, in spite of your protests that burning a fully grown fruit-bearing nabuk tree was considered a portent of doom by the people of Baghdad.

Your day starts in your black leather chair. Your room is larger than your old one. There are more shelves. Beside you is a small table covered with tablets and medication. Hiding behind the sphygmomanometer is a glass, half filled with water; a mercury thermometer appears bent inside it. The phone is by your side; you ring up people whose names I've heard before. Some of them I know; others I've never met. They send a driver out from the project to collect you two or three times a week. The rest of your days are spent with those multicolored materials, which keep you preoccupied till the early hours of the morning. You place them in large containers and send them off. You then receive other parcels at the end of each month, and so on. Sometimes you offer to drop me at school with the driver before heading down the farm road toward the industrial area.

I come back to find you waiting for me in the garden. You're laying out a new bed of roses, or scattering parsley seeds in a square patch of dark soil. When I start my piano practice every evening, you're again in the garden, thinning out the hedge, or relieving the trunk of a young orange tree of a parasitic vine that is choking it. If I stop my practicing for a few brief moments, I hear you calling to me from the window, "Where have you drifted off to?" You like to hear me practice for a whole hour without any interruptions. When we discuss my school dance lessons, you say to me, "You'll develop muscles, and your body will look like a man's." You insist on describing my future in dance as "impending masculinity," hoping that your criticism will put me off, thus achieving your dream that I become a pianist.

However, you rapidly changed your mind when I called out to my mother later that week, refusing adamantly to let you enter my room instead of her. When she arrived, with all the whiteness of her skin, I was crying in my bed. She placed her hand on my head, ruffling my shining hair. I didn't calm down; I lay there with my legs slightly parted. I was going to have to take off my underpants with her there. I couldn't remember the last time I'd undressed in her presence. I showed her my white cotton pants with the spot of blood in the center that had frightened me so much. She smiled with a calmness that infuriated me. I'm dying and she's smiling! She went out and came back with a bag of soft paper tissues and half a dozen cotton pads. She told me how to use them to avoid soiling myself, then sat for a quarter of an hour at the edge of the bed explaining what was happening to me. It was the longest quarter of an hour of my life! Didn't Khaddouja die when her blood drained from her body? I then became afraid that I would face death every month. I never forgave my mother for not preparing me for this day. She walked out of my room and said to you, "Your daughter's periods have started."

So I continued with my muscular dance lessons. I often danced along that corridor in our new home. Sometimes, I was Cinderella, at other times I was Coppelia or the Dying Swan. The electricity wires running along the wall were festive ribbons, and the steel nails were the eyes of the admiring audience. The patches of peeling paint were exploding fireworks as I bent and stretched—"Plié, relevé"—like a frog on the doorstep of my mother's kitchen. I often tried to imitate the way she walked on a cushion of air. She's smoking while she's waiting for the water to boil. I ask her, "What are you cooking?" She answers without turning around, "Pasta." Before I can stop myself, I've exclaimed, "Again!" I see her standing there tied up with ropes of spaghetti, her hair hanging with coils of it, spaghetti worms crawling from her ears. She boils her miseries in a pressure cooker. She doesn't have the time to spend many hours preparing varied meals. Her work takes up most of her time.

The valve on the pressure cooker whistles, accompanying her hoarse operatic attempts, lost in the corners of the house amid the bristles of her daily sweeping. I still remember my first punishment, her angry scolding, for mocking her awful singing when I told her that I would grow up to be a singer like her. She later regretted what she'd said and apologized. But she didn't hesitate in punishing me again, and more forcefully, when I fell behind in my ballet training. She sent me back to the dance studio, and the kitchen door was always shut in my face; extra meals were forbidden. She explained to me firmly, "It's to maintain your figure." That's why I eat like a pig when I'm angry or upset! A habit that almost ruined my figure. I nearly stopped going into the dance studio with its paneled mirrors; they made me feel more shy and self-conscious as I padded about in my burst training stockings. My days continued like this until you asked me to join you in your bedroom on a Friday evening. My mother had gone out with Millie. You said, "Why don't you come and help me with my experiments? I'm feeling bored today."

Those hours that started with your boredom were an experiment in themselves. You said the boredom was set off by the Egyptian film on television that started at four. It was always followed by the classic song "Shams al-Aseel"— "Sunset," by the eminent Egyptian singer Um Kalthoum— and then the religious programs. It was this sequence that made you feel down. You asked, "How can this machine be so powerful in programming depression like this?" After a long sigh, you suggested to me: "Come on, live for today, we're not the masters of tomorrow. Let's have a cup of coffee and talk." That was the first time I was allowed to drink coffee. It was also the first time I crossed my legs and listened. You offered me a small amount of freedom in that room's atmosphere, saying to me:

—My daughter, listen to me, and learn how to listen to others. I'm telling you this today because you've started to grow up. I can start depending on you. I feel there is so much I want to talk to you about. I want you to remember what I'm telling you about the art of listening, because it will stay with you longer than degrees, ballet, music, numbers, and even memories. Did you know that the sense of hearing is the last one we lose when we die?

I didn't know if you were talking to me or to yourself. You were sipping the coffee that you'd been banned from drinking during your recovery. I was fearful of this first lesson. When you invited me to join you in your experiments, I felt that I'd outgrown my braid. I could see a world I'd never dreamt I'd enter with you, a world of senses so different from what I encountered in my classrooms and dance studios. It's your domain, which my mother describes as sticky and chaotic—the bags, tubes, containers, boxes, beakers, cylinders, research studies, laboratory samples, food additives, flavors, scents, and fragrances that surround us in all directions. You opened a door, leading me toward creativity and excellence. But you were full of skepticism about my ability to listen. You said to me:

—Close your eyes. I'll place something under your nose. Smell it, see if you can identify it and its color.

I sat up straight, waiting for the game to start. You held something with an acidic smell close to my face and asked me:

—What is it?

I replied:

—I think it's a lemon.

—What else?

I continued:

—Its color is yellow, of course.

—Taste it, then.

I tasted the substance and said:

—No, it can't be a lemon, it must be an orange; it has a sweet taste to it.

—Well, taste it again, then.

I tasted it again.

—Yes, it must be an orange.

—So open your eyes now, my little one, and let us see.

I read the label on the plastic container that contained the powder I'd been smelling: PINK CITRUS, ESSENCE OF FLOWER, GHOSTLY BUD.

I laughed aloud. I was surprised at all these names. You said to me:

—Do you see now? It's not an orange or a lemon. It's a synthetic substance made from citrus fruits. I've given it these names. What do you think? Which one is the most suitable? I have to choose a name for it and send it back to the lab this week so they can decide on the substance's final name.

—Why do you have to do that?

—Because it's my job, and I love it. I'm a trader in flavorings. My dear, God has given me a gift, which is a highly developed sense of taste and smell, which not many people have. I've specialized in this field after having worked in it for several years. I can now create unusual names for the foods, flavors, and fragrances that we synthesize in the lab. I smell and taste the substances, analyze their colors, and ponder over their appropriate names. It may take me several nights to come up with the right name for the taste or scent. That is where the magic begins.

—I didn't know that that was what you spent your time doing in your room. Is that why you hate my mother's smoke?

—Exactly, my dear. The smoke damages the delicate membranes that contain the smell fibers inside the nostrils. Your mother doesn't understand what I do. I no longer care that she doesn't understand. But I've asked you here today to see if you'd be interested in sharing my profession. I'll open a new set of containers for you every week, and we'll sit together, contemplate the materials, and name them. In other words, I want to make you my companion in these endeavors. I've started to feel lonely when the evening comes, even though I enjoy listening to the melodies you play while I work.

I don't know what to answer. Suddenly you're offering me the chance to become your work companion. You take my hand and squeeze it gently. I feel tickled by a strange new sensation. It resembles the pink citrus taste you tested me with. A friendship that is larger than me has been thrust upon me unexpectedly in the afternoon. I will have to grow into it!

My mother didn't work for the petrol company as she'd planned. She found alternative employment working for Middle East Airlines in Sa'adoun Street, near Semiramis Cinema. When she gets home, it's past three o'clock in the afternoon; she melts into the cool breeze from the air cooler. She spends more than two hours drifting in her sacred sleep. Her mood when she awakes is marred only by your pointing out that she spends too much time sleeping and that the sun has started to set. Each and every day you make the same complaint:

—You spend half the day asleep. If you're not used to working, then give it up! Or instead of sleeping in the afternoon, go to bed earlier in the evening.

She snaps back at you:

—Please don't interfere in this matter. When I sleep and when I get up is my business!

The tension in your voices starts to climb the scale upward.

—Do you ever ask yourself who is with the girl in the afternoons? She spends the whole day studying, while you're out looking for pastes that tan the skin within half an hour, powders that hide your wrinkles, bleaches to hide your blemishes, preparations to tighten your facial skin, hand-softening creams, oils for damaged hair, and you've even learned how to prepare pastes to remove unwanted hair at home! What's happened to you since we moved to the city?

—You are what's happened to me! Your presence in the house has driven me to go out for as many hours as possible. My daughter's growing up; she no longer needs my attention as she did when she was smaller. Don't try to play on my conscience. I have no guilt about working and fulfilling my duties at home. So don't try any emotional blackmail with me. She's fine and she misses nothing!

—You've also become very glib. This is what I feared. How I wish that I wasn't restricted by the doctor's instructions, then I could offer her all that she lacks. I curse the day I blacked out!

—You always turn everything I do into a drama!

I'm watching my mother. As she opens her lips to answer back, she reveals her teeth, little bulges, the size of almonds in a row. When she talks, her tonsils move like those of a soprano; they resonate and seem to me like two vibrating tamarind seeds.

She continues:

—I don't like to be criticized, you know that very well. I can offer no more than this, especially in this cursed heat. Isn't it enough that I have to put up with these endless power cuts?

She wanders off, looking for a traditional straw fan, since she's lost her Spanish lace fan. After a few moments of silence, you tell her, as though nothing has happened:

—If you soak it in water, it will give you a cooler breeze.

Then you leave the room.

I, too, turned around, heading toward my room. My mother can't bear it when her cheeks become red and swollen and her body starts to sweat. She eventually returns to her bed, half-naked. She's adamant that she'll become dehydrated, that one day she will die, dried out. I agree with her on that point, I'm thinking to myself as I climb the stairs. She wasn't born in a hot climate like me. The heat of our summer, as they say, evaporates the blood from underneath the skin. The temperature today, according to the media, is 40 degrees Centigrade in the shade. Everyone says that the media are lying, that if they told the truth, admitting how hot it really was, all daily activities would cease and everything would close down.

My loneliness intensified that evening. The fan's whirring ceases—another power cut! I'm left with the heat and the dark. I light a candle and gaze at its flame, forgetting my studies. I slam my book shut in frustration. A mosquito has fallen into the cup of tea by the candle. I lift it out with my pencil tip and cast it aside. I drink what's left in the cup; then I catch another one. Something makes me want to trap it. I place it on the book in front of me and cut off its wings, crushing its limbs with my pen. I feel as though I possess it. I wonder, do we possess other living creatures and then torture them? Or do we torture them in order to feel that we possess them? The minutes pass slowly, as if time actually makes a sound during the heat, and you can feel it passing by you slowly. Suddenly I feel guilty because of what I've done to this creature. The mosquito has made me feel pity. What if its soul came back and it sought revenge? What if it became as big as the room and did to me what I'd done to it? To chase my superstitious fears away, I tried to stick its wings back onto its body, the delicate head back where it belonged. I'd almost completed my satanic experiment by candlelight when the electric current suddenly came back on, restarting the tall floor fan that stood in front of me, and its gust of wind blew the mosquito and its amputated segments into my face. It all happened in a split second, before I'd realized what was going on. The mosquito had its revenge as I shouted out in a terrified, hoarse voice, "Oh, Mother!"

I went downstairs to the kitchen to look for a bag of mixed seeds: grilled sunflower seeds, fried melon seeds and roasted watermelon seeds, white seeds, red seeds, striped seeds. It's time to go to sleep. I'll sit on my metal, summer bed on the flat rooftop and devour the seeds as I gaze up at the stars. I once tried to count all of them as I lay on my back. I carried on eating until I finished a whole bag of seeds. I had a terrible stomachache later that night, but I didn't dare tell my mother. Now I put on my lightest dishdasha and my rubber thongs. I turned off the light by the door leading onto the rooftop, to keep away the insects, and lay down on my humid cotton mattress. I lie on one side for at least ten minutes, allowing the other side to become cool and moist. I then roll over exposing the patch underneath me, which has become hot, to the cool breeze, and so on. I wish that cursed bat would fly away instead of circling overhead. People say that bats cling to the face and suck out our blood through the eyes. I cover my face until I fall asleep.

Some evenings, when everything evaporates in the heat, even sleepiness, I leave the light by the entrance to the rooftop switched on, and I amuse myself by watching a lizard catching mosquitoes and ants with its tongue. It resembles a flattened frog. After a while I get bored watching it and strike it hard with my slipper. The ugly reptile, with its transparent blue veins, hurries away, leaving behind its moist tail, which is dancing on its own on the ground by the door's edge. The next morning, one greedy fly is all it takes to wake me up, or it might be the sound of the cooing pigeons that are watching me from their perches on the drainpipe, or from the higher rooftop above the storeroom at the side of the stairs. Sometimes I've been wakened before that by the sound of the call to prayers from the mosque nearby. I awake comforted and secure at dawn in the shade of the majestic evergreen tree in the center of the garden. My mother can't understand why I insist on sleeping on the rooftop. How can I explain to her that the vastness of the velvety sky overhead, with the scattered diamonds, takes me closer to Khaddouja?

Another week begins. The scenario starts with my folding the cotton mattress in half and taking it into the storeroom away from the heat of the midday sun. The room is full of rolled-up carpets that have been stuffed with mothballs and wrapped away. We won't be using them again until winter returns. I enter the bathroom to wash away the sweat of the night before, then pick up my toothbrush. A large ant is trying to maintain its balance as it attempts to negotiate the nylon bristles. It looks happy to me, licking the toothpaste residue on the brush. I pick up the brush and shake it off. The miserable creature falls into the washbasin. I turn on the tap and drown it in the froth. It disappears quickly down the plughole.

I look at myself in the mirror. My brown skin is contrasted against the white tiles behind me. I see some fuzz on my upper lip. I have to learn from my mother this technique she's picked up to remove unwanted hair using a thread. I was watching her a few days ago. She attached one end of the spool to the handle of a window near where she was sitting. She inserted three fingers halfway down the length of the thread and twirled it around them, creating a triangle that slid across her skin, plucking away the unwanted hairs as the crossover point moved up and down. She moves her head backward and forward, as though she is swinging her neck to the rhythm of a subtle oriental melody. My mother is learning quickly in the city what she refused for a long time when we lived in the country. And you, Father, continue to tease her—"Now my wife has learned the art of plucking hair!" I run the soiled brush over my teeth; the taste of mint overwhelms me. My mother refuses to let me remove my fuzz the way she does when I ask her.

Coming down the stairs as I head toward the breakfast table, I step on a red cockroach or a black beetle that has fallen onto its back unable to right itself all night. It makes a dry crunching sound underneath my feet. Its delicate feelers wriggle about until they're crushed. The ants then arrive and gratefully carry away the fragmented remains. You pick up the comb to plait my braid in the kitchen. Suddenly you pull on it tightly. "What's this, my daughter? Did you fall asleep last night with chewing gum in your mouth? Bubble gum, by the looks of it!" Without any further discussion, my mother has picked up the scissors and snipped off the tip of my braid. About a week later, she convinced me to get rid of the whole braid by saying, "It's too hot to be walking around with all that hair." I agreed. I pick up a small fragrant white razki flower that I find floating in half a centimeter of water in a small saucer. I fix it to the buttonhole of my shirt before I leave.

They say that a child can't comprehend the concept of "routine." Why is it, then, that I've started to feel it? I must have become an older child. I've become bored with the lessons I'm taught at school. I've put on some weight, and that has made me less keen about my dance lessons. Whenever I feel stressed, I eat more. I can no longer bear to listen to my mother's advice, or to the piano teacher when he tells me off for neglecting to practice. The six days of the week have become an inevitable chore that I have to endure until Thursday comes around. Then I use the water hose to wash down the veranda in front of the house, and the rooftop. I'll water the garden, then watch the evening film on television, then devour the contents of the glossy *Samar* teenage magazine.

I say goodbye to my mother at sundown from the back door, when she hears the tooting of David and Millie's car horn. She walks out on tiptoe, trying to stop her high heels from sinking into the mud pillows where you had planted some mint seedlings that morning. You enjoy the leaves with your cup of tea, or on a slice of the local white cheese. I watch their greeting ritual from where I'm standing by the garden tap. The car stops, David gets out, giving my mother a hug and a wide smile. Millie gets out of the front seat quickly, vacating it for my mother, then takes up her place in the back seat quite happily. Another brief hug before the car moves off. A quick glance backward from my mother. She looks toward me, but doesn't see me.

I spend Friday finishing my school homework. I then clean my glass fish tank and change its water. I watch the dancing many-colored, scaly creatures inside it. I speak to them but get no reply. Eyes without lashes stare back at me through the glass; they're continuously sending out kisses and bubbles. We had river fish and rice for lunch. In the afternoon depression sets in, until we dispel it with the flavorings game.

Together we prepare a bag of popcorn and take it up to your room. You say to me:

—Today we'll be working only with colors, which is why I allowed you to eat the popcorn, as its salty taste would spoil your ability to pick out the various flavors. This week I received a contract from a new company that produces paints and emulsions. They want to compete in the local market and have asked me to come up with unusual and exotic names for them, and to give them suggestions for how to promote their products. I want you to help me. Today we need to let our imagination go free, to the end of the rainbow.

—What about tasting the products? I've been looking forward to that all week!

—There are many projects, my little one, and there will be a lot of that in the weeks to come. Now, let us start work.

You take out the largest collection of colored squares I've seen in my life. Meters of samples, shades that can't be imagined. Fluorescent ribbons, shiny ones, and others with rough surfaces wait for us to give them names. Rectangles, triangles, and circles of color compete in the degree of their purity. We spread them out on the floor in your room and start with the most appealing ones. You point to the first color and ask me:

—So what do you think, my assistant, what is this?

I reply without any hesitation:

—Blue.

—What name do you want it to have?

I thought for a while:

—Light blue.

You laugh and your eyes sparkle.

—No, no, no . . . that's no good. I'll give you an example. It's like: the Spray from the Ocean, the Blue of Dolphins, a Silver Mist, Dry Ice. The name has to be poetic and unusual. That is the secret! Don't you think?

I read your glinting eyes and reply:

—Exactly, but how are we going to come up with names like that for all these other colors?

—Don't worry, they'll come. Now look at this color—
what is it called?

—Orange.

—That's not enough. It could be called Inspiration of
Rust, Desert Bronze, Golden Honey, Fragments of Autumn.

I was astonished. I didn't know what to say. You start to
make some notes in your little book. I put some popcorn in
my mouth and gaze at you.

—This is a pretty color, it's a pleasant brown. Let's call it
Bleached Brown, Dust from the Little Mountains, Eastern
Spice, or Crusty Bread. What do you think?

—Excellent.

—It's your turn now with this color.

—I see it as a Spot of Shiny White.

—Very good, and I see it as Angel's Wings, Oyster's Pearl,
Waterfall's Froth, or an Ice Cave.

I laughed,

—In this heat, Father?

—Hmm, you have a point. You see, you've started to
associate the color with the name.

You then pick up a yellowish brown color and say:

—I defy you to name this color.

I reply:

—Caramel.

You add:

—Or maybe Dusky Skin, or Wild Mushroom Peel.

I couldn't keep up with your wealth of ideas. I preferred
to just listen.

—Don't give up. You'll learn how to do this very quickly.
I'm sure of that. This yellow color, what do you think?

—A lemon.

—Yes, but it's an impure yellow. It could be called Pineapple Scales, or Banana Mousse.

—But Father, these colors are paints!

—That's what makes it more exciting.

Each name takes at least ten minutes of thinking. Sometimes it takes you more than half an hour to choose a certain name. It's only now that I'm getting to know you. This secret world of yours had never dawned on me. I'd been engrossed in my school routine, my uniform, and my training. I never thought that I could imagine the color pink as Cherry Gel, or that I could call the color green a Lazy Forest, a Fermented Apple Skin, or a River Pebble. How do you come up with such magic, Father? Is this what my mother meant when she said that you seduced her with your descriptions of the East?

The weeks pass; we compete to find new names for our colors. Fridays have become less depressing. We giggle at the breakfast table when you cut through a boiled egg and say:

—Ah, a Grainy Yolk.

I reply:

—No, it's Woven Amber.

You cry out:

—You cheeky girl; the professor's student has become a professor and a half!

My mother casts a bemused look in our direction from behind her newspaper. She lifts up her knife. It has some dark berry jam on it. She spreads it on her slice of toast. I turn toward you.

—Baba, what do you think?

You say with a smile:

—A Turkish Plum.

I say:

—No, Wild Berries.

You add:

—Well done, but it's more like a Unique Grape.

I say:

—No, that's a very ordinary name. What about Ground Ruby?

You reply:

—Excellent.

It was thus that we colored our days. We spent a whole evening on the shades of the color gray. I'd never seen such beauty before. I say to you:

—How do they make these colors in the laboratories?

—Science and technology are constantly making great advances. If we learn how to put science to good use, the future for humankind holds great promise.

You suggested to me:

—Volcanic Ash, Gray Cloud.

—Did you not say that we should avoid using the name of the color itself?

—Yes, but gray is not a color; it's a puzzling nuance.

—Alright, then, Smoky Haze.

—Well done, or Froth on the Beach, Powdered Stone.

I jump up and shout:

—Yes, Powdered Stone fits perfectly, as if it's the color of concrete.

—I think you'll excel in this field, my little one.

—Does that mean I'll have to study chemistry like you, Baba?

—You may not need to do that if you want to remain my

assistant. Anyway, this is just some preliminary experience for you. There are specialized courses in the field of advertising that you may want to do when you grow up.

I ask you:

—What about Seal's Fur?

You reply:

—That will be its trade name. You've now registered a color in your name for the first time.

You take me into the world of colors and flavors—some of them lived in my dreams; some dwelled, with all their crystals, under my tongue.

You look up at the clock on the wall. It's past one o'clock. You say:

—My God, I forgot that you have to go to school tomorrow. Hurry up and get ready for bed.

I kiss you, leaving you in your room. My mother's room is totally silent.

That night, for the first time, I awoke from my sleep, startled. I could hear my mother shouting downstairs, at three-thirty in the morning, and you're shouting at the top of your voice:

—It seems I've given you too many liberties, which you don't deserve!

—I don't care what you say. I'm fed up with this sham relationship. I enjoy spending my evenings with my foreign friends, staying up late with them; I will not let you spoil it for me when I get back. I'm not Cinderella—I don't have to be back by midnight. Can't you understand that my life is now separate from yours? We don't live together, nor do we even get along together, we merely reside in the same house!

—As long as you live in this house, you'll respect its traditions. I don't think I've left you lacking for anything.
Don't make our lives more confused.

—So we're back to it's all my fault. Can't you understand? I want a final separation. I don't want your favors,
nor do I want you to remind me that you're the master of
this house. I'm content with my job, my friends, and my
daughter.

—Where will you live? In Basra?

—Why not? Isn't it better than this hell I'm living in now?

—You don't even bother to deny your relationship with
him!

At this point I felt you were going to explode with anger.
I could hear crying. You threw something at her. It was the
ashtray. It struck my glass fish tank with a crack. I could
hear the water start to trickle out from it slowly.

You were coughing violently, you were saying:

—If this is what you want, woman, then I'll divorce you.
You can have what you want. Go to him, or go back to England! The child is mine, she'll stay with me, I promise you
that. The law is on my side. I'll keep it on my side whether
you like it or not!

I could hear my mother's footsteps coming up the stairs.
She was panting as she went past my door. I held my breath
until I heard you, too, going back to your room. It was my
first experience with insomnia. Barefoot, I crept down to
the room where the argument had taken place. The beautiful creatures were thrashing about. One of my goldfish had
died. It was floating above the bubbles released from its
companions. The water was dripping from the side of the
tank; a little puddle had formed underneath it. I pulled out

the plug and the air pump went silent. I picked up the tank; it was no longer that heavy, as it was now only half full of water, which had already become cloudy. As I picked it up, the water swung about inside it, and the pairs of goldfish peered at me. I headed toward the bathroom and pushed the door open with my foot. I glanced into the toilet bowl. Two small turds were floating in the water. They reminded me of the color of my skin. I thought to myself, Chocolate Soap, then chided myself for the thought. I emptied the contents of the tank into the toilet and pushed the metal handle down. Tsshh! I gulped. I stood there for a moment thinking about what I'd done. Then I walked out of the bathroom and shut the door behind me.

THE GAME OF COLORS; the challenge of flavorings; the imagination of fragrances; the magic of odors: all that no longer mattered. The confrontations increased. I started to get used to your problems. Whereas in the past I used to run with them to my room, now I'd learned to stay where I was and listen without interfering. After a period of trying, I'd reached a stage at which I no longer heard the commotion. Like the magnet in the sewing box that I used to collect the scattered pins. The first pin makes an audible click, so does the second and the third, until the entire magnetic surface is smothered with pins. Then they stick to each other without making any sound. Eventually, the pinheads start to drop, due to their excessive weight. That's the way I learned to drop problems that weighed me down. It was a situation that my mother hated. I felt that she wanted me on her side at the time of her greatest distress, but I couldn't decide who the victim was.

You offer me a milky white powder, saying:

—In the lab, they want to call this Soda Cream. Common and familiar, don't you think? What would you suggest? Sweet Marble?

I reply:

—That's pretty, but is it truly sweet, or is that just the name of the color?

—It will be used as flavoring in cakes. What about Slivers of Shells?

I say:

—Slivers of Shells is a gentle poetic name, but it doesn't work for a cake powder. Baba, let us not escape over the rainbow. If there truly were a pot of gold at the end of it, like there is in Mother's fairy tales, I'd understand your insistence. But now you possess the pot, isn't that so?

You sigh and sit on a chair near to me, saying:

—Yes, my daughter, I've worked very hard. I've achieved more than I dreamed I could in my lifetime. I must also admit that your mother was right when she insisted that you should go to school in the city. I didn't want to be selfish when our financial situation improved. This house we now live in is only the beginning. But . . .

I move closer to you, saying:

—I want to speak to you about that "But." I'm no longer the child you think I am. You have to tell me what is at the end of this road.

You answer me as though the words are a burden you're getting off your chest.

—I don't know, my little one. She wants a final separation. For me, that's called a divorce. But that's not in our best interest—to be specific, that's not in your best interest. Can you imagine us getting divorced after all these years? But then, I can't allow her to go out all over the place with the foreigners the way she wants to. She travels from Baghdad to Basra; she tells me she's going—not to ask for my permission, merely to inform me. I can't allow anyone to make a mockery of me.

I ask you anxiously:

—So what will you do, Father?

You answer me with a little sadness.

—Were I not at risk for another heart attack, I'd arrange for us all to move to England. But this is my homeland, and we've prospered here. I don't want us to end up in the cultural void I endured during my student days. The thought of living far from my homeland again frightens me. I tell you that quite frankly.

You look at me and a smile crosses your face. You add:

—My God, don't little girls grow up quickly!

—Have you forgotten that my sixteenth birthday is next month?

You strike your forehead, saying:

—You make us age with you!

We exchange a hug. You then take out a thin card from your pocket. Its color is that of apricots which will ripen in a week's time. You say:

—Go on. Show me how clever you are.

—Melon Juice.

—I called it Dance of the Salmon.

—Very nice, Father. I'll give you another alternative—Cold Coral.

You wink at me, saying:

—It truly is a Cold Coral.

—When will you start working shorter hours? The haggard look on your face worries me.

—There's nothing in my life other than these hours of fantasy, and this work; were it not for that, I would have died a long time ago.

Suddenly you stop as you remember something else.

—By the way, I want you to take your mother to our neighbor's mourning ceremony. Um Nidhal's husband has died. He was very good to me when he was alive. We must perform our duty as neighbors.

—I'll tell Mother, and we'll go tomorrow.

—Don't forget to take a few yards of black cloth as a gift for his widow.

You then add in a forceful tone:

—I don't need to remind you, it would be most improper to leave before dinner is served!

On this day, all the women are draped in black as they gather in a circle surrounding Um Nidhal, mother of Nidhal; like all old ladies, she is referred to as the mother of her eldest-born child. The hired cleric chants verses from the Koran, droning in the corridor outside that leads to the kitchen. The fortune-teller is bursting the evil eye from the depths of the cup of Arabic coffee. Its sediment is like brown asphalt in the bottom of the cup. I gaze at the group of women, huddled black bats, weeping over the passing of Abu Nidhal, father of Nidhal. I remember him well. He used to complain to you about his wife's behavior and the way she welcomed all the beggars in our area: "I tell her, dearest Um Nidhal, I have asked you a thousand times, please don't bring these people into our house. That old woman with a humped back who offers to remove women's unwanted body hair, or the 'Ten Fils' beggar, the one who refuses any charity unless it's a ten-fils coin, and Crazy Hassan who rides around on his red bicycle, offering to repair people's televisions; and the worst of the lot, Majda, the servant who walks around barefoot, carrying her slippers under her arm, or hanging around her neck on a piece of string."

I enter the big reception hall with Millie and my mother. Millie knew the daughter, Nidhal, from the days before we'd moved to the city. We leave our shoes in a pile by the entrance—a smell of fish bones wafts up from it. We greet the dead man's closest relatives. They're sitting in a straight row, so that the visiting women know who to offer their condolences to. It's preferable for the grieving widow not to change the position where she sits from the first day till the seventh. A change in position could lead to a confrontation with stern glances. The women enter. A variety of sizes, heights, shapes, dimensions, complexions, features, and ages. They all wear a traditional black abaya. Through the abaya's small opening, each face peers out in turn to cast a comprehensive glance, gauging the mood in the room. When the elderly women sit down on the mattresses laid out on the floor, their abayas widen out at the sides in a parachuting effect, hiding their rounded figures. They look like sacks of rice that have been scattered around in sorrow.

One of the seated women says, "My dears, the mourning has cooled down!" It's difficult to determine who's the mullaya—the leading person at a women's mourning ceremony—until she raises her voice and starts to chant. A young woman goes up to the cleric reading the Koran, saying to him, "Please, the women want to chant." He shakes his head in disapproval. He stops reading from the Koran and asks God for his forgiveness. His head protrudes from his skeletal body. The green turban he's wearing has a white ribbon all around it; he looks like a pencil with an eraser on its tip. The mullaya takes over and starts to wail, "What sorrow has befallen you, O master of this house!" Her companion nudges her with an elbow. "It's the master of the house who has died," she whispers. The mullaya corrects herself. "What sorrow has befallen you all with the loss of the Master of this house!"

The words have their effect on Um Nidhal. She starts to sob as though she's just been informed of her husband's death at that moment. The sound of the women's crying grows louder. "Why, Abu Nidhal, why have you gone and left us?" Another woman cries out, "Your time had not come, Abu Nidhal," as she strikes her thigh in a continuous rhythm. I imagine them all as a group of mourning widows comforting each other. One of the women had reputedly not left her home since the day she lost her son. She came here today to relive her sorrow and to do her duty toward her neighbor. The sound of the women's wailing grows louder. Each one of them is reliving the tale of her departed one: this woman's loved one drowned, the other was struck down by a speeding car, another had been burned to death when the gas canister in her kitchen exploded. It was a public call for weeping!

One of the women tells her daughter to readjust her hijab, the Islamic veil. "Cover your hair, my daughter."

When the abaya slips off the head of one of the women, I can see the groove between her two breasts just below her neckline. The area is all red from the forceful blows where she's been hitting herself, overcome with the emotion of the moment, like a beat hammered out on a silenced drum. My mother asks Millie, "Why all this torture? Isn't it enough that they've lost a loved one?" Millie replies, "Don't be surprised, it's their tradition. They say it's healthier this way. They stir themselves up with the wailing and beating their chests and get rid of all their stifled sorrows in one session. They don't break it up into portions and come down with depression at a later date."

A queue of young women has formed, tall and slim, like sticks of black charcoal, extending from the kitchen to where the women guests are seated. They're preparing a pastry with dates and vegetable oil. It will be distributed among the poor on behalf of the dead man's soul. One woman turns to her companion, murmuring, "Did you see what she looks like without any makeup on? Her skin is like leftover soup!" They cover their faces with their abayas to muffle the sound of their hushed giggles. One of them sucks on a cardamom seed; the other is chewing on some dried carnation buds. Heyla, their black servant woman, comes into the kitchen with her big belly and wide hips. The girls realize that the kitchen has become too crowded and withdraw meltingly, like boiled okra fingers. I like Heyla's kindness. She calls out to one of the seated women, a veterinarian who'd been talking to her friend about chick incubators, the vaccines chicks needed, and the various viruses that had spread recently, affecting the newly hatched. The vet comes into the kitchen. I would like to change Heyla's ancient name—it means cardamom—and call her Um al-Abid, or Mother of the Dark Servant, the trade name of a local chocolate biscuit.

Soon after that, the trays are brought in: silver, gilded, plastic, old and new, imported, borrowed, and hired. The coffee cups used on these occasions differ from the ones used on happy occasions. The coffee cup used at these sad ceremonies has no handle, and in its bottom half is the tarry, bitter liquid. One of the women asks for her cup to be refilled. A younger one provides her with more of the required stimulant. She is wearing a chain around her neck. From it dangles an image of the Ka'aba—the sacred Muslim shrine—in black and gold. The only makeup she wears is black eyeliner from Mecca. She says that all other beauty products are forbidden in Islamic law. The other women are all covered by their abayas from head to toe. I catch a brief glimpse of the hand of one of the women as she withdraws it rapidly lest anyone notices the nail polish that she's failed to remove. She's either forgotten about it, or run out of polish remover, or maybe a friend borrowed her bottle and failed to give it back.

I hear gentle whimpering from one direction, and louder crying from another. Some women are sniffling in a delicate, cultured way, whereas the neighbor's daughter is releasing her sorrows in an uninhibited manner, with no embarrassment. A diplomat's wife is sitting on a chair, tickling the tip of her nose using a scented handkerchief with embroidered edges. The neighbor's daughter pinches her nose with a paper tissue, almost distorting it. The crying of the woman who has lived abroad differs from the crying of the family's midwife, who delivers their pregnant daughters' babies. A fat woman wears a blue turquoise ring she has inherited from previous generations; the diplomat's wife has forgotten to remove her diamond ring. One of the seated women insists that there are only slivers of diamond in it. She swears that the mullaya's gold tooth is worth more.

I glance toward Millie. She's talking with my mother, telling her the story of her friend Ann, who lived in the North of England. She had her husband cremated when he died, and kept his ashes. She had them placed in an hourglass, which she put on a shelf in her kitchen. She turned it over twice every day. She would watch the grains moving from the upper chamber to the lower one and talk to them, saying, "I'm sorry, dear husband, you never worked your entire life. Your laziness drove me crazy, so I decided to make you do something now that you're dead." She would then make the sign of the cross, asking the Virgin Mary to forgive him. And her!

The conflicting smells were stifling me—the incense, and the kubba being fried in the kitchen. The nylon socks leave a red band around the women's ankles in the heat. Everything is black except for the colorful tissue boxes being handed out here and there. The women start having cramps in their legs for sitting too long on the ground. The whiteness of the tissues is flowing as their boxes go from hand to hand, trade names are circulating: Flowers, Perfumes, Springtime, Water Droplets, Green Grass, and Breeze, followed by the printed statement "One hundred 2-ply tissues." Um Nidhal is gazing blankly at the pattern on the carpet. There's some froth at the side of her mouth. She's not aware of what's happening around her. I make my excuses and head outside through the back door of the kitchen.

A sheep has been tied to a tree in the garden. Its teeth look almost human as it chews away incessantly. The gardener approaches, followed by the butcher, who has come out with his knife. "Baaa." The fearful animal has started to produce black pellets; they emerge from its backside and tumble to the ground around it. The sheep and I exchange glances just as the two men grab it by its hide and lift it up. They throw the sheep onto its side, and its quivering tail falls into the mud beneath it. The butcher grabs its head and pulls it backward. The animal's eyes roll upward. The mound of wool quivers as the butcher murmurs, "In the name of God, the Merciful, the Compassionate." A wide, smiling gash opens up in the animal's neck and a red fluid gushes out. They collect it in a large bowl as they hold the sheep down on its side. Then the bowl containing its life's blood is pushed aside. A swarm of flies descends on it. I can almost make out their hairy legs stained with sheep's blood. The two men squat down. The gardener holds up one of the animal's hind legs, and the butcher makes a small hole in the animal's hide, in the upper part of the thigh. The elastic skin separates easily around this new opening. Human breath will soon enter the animal's body through this fresh hole. "Blow into the sheep from here!" They take turns breathing into the carcass. My lungs fill up as I hold my breath, watching their foreheads redden. A flicker of black spots clouds my view of the scene. They bring a rope. They hang the bloated corpse up from its hind legs—an offering to the passing of the dead man. Its head dangles loosely, almost severed from the rest of its body.

And you asked me not to leave until dinner had been served!

The sharp knife flits across the dark pink tissues. The entrails hang out, loops of serpents, weighing down the branch the dead sheep is hanging from. The process of skinning the animal disgusts me! As I close my eyes, I glimpse a bed of white razki flowers. The contents of the bowl have been poured onto the soil around them. It's said that these flowers will be revitalized by the blood. Gardenias flourish when iron filings are buried in their soil. I could taste that rust in my mouth. I feel a strange dizziness. I see visions of snapdragons and flowers that look like cats' paws, others that look like clock faces, more flowers that seem shy and withdrawn. One of the women calls me in, as dinner has been served. The women have started gathering around the large table. I gaze at their backs from where I'm standing. They're like pairs of crows in their abayas, pecking at the food with their beaks. I hear a stout woman whispering to her companion, "Poor Um Nidhal, she doesn't deserve what has befallen her." She swallows down the contents of a large spoonful of yellow-colored rice. An elderly woman wearing dark glasses answers, "She'll get accustomed to her grief, just as the eye gets accustomed to the dark." She bites into a piece of crusty bread. I feel a dryness in my throat, as if I've swallowed some raw grains of wheat without any water.

The morning sun tickles my feet, waking me up. I wash in cold water and come down the stairs from the roof. The dawn's early light follows me down to the kitchen. The house is hushed and quiet, in contrast to the sound of your recent arguments, which had made it as noisy as the coppersmiths' market. I wander out into the garden with a cup of tea in my hand and a fragrant cube of Turkish delight. I walk barefoot through the grass, lost in my thoughts. I sit down on the last step leading to the garden, folding my feet up underneath me. I watch a cat digging up the soft earth to deposit its litter in the pit it has created. It then rubs its fur against the trunk of the palm tree. Its tail is pointing upward and quivering. I'm tempted to drench it with the hose, but that would stir up the mosquitoes hiding among the leaves of the tree behind it, and the flies. I no longer play those childish games I used to so enjoy: Kash Keesh and the elastic rope game, Kibbi and Touki (the stone and jumping game), Shabateet (the longer-breath competition), Police and Burglars, and the Hunt the Gazelle game. Next week I'll go on a strict diet to lose some weight. You pointed out to me that I was now a little taller, and you suggested that I should regulate what I eat from now on. I'm waiting for you to provide me with a diet list for the coming week. To encourage me you promised that you would join me in my diet, and together we would regain our fitness.

Suddenly I hear the sound of a car speeding down the road and a squeal of brakes outside our gate. I leave my cup of tea and run. One of the local youths has stolen his father's car. He has run over the unfortunate cat as he sped away. The animal has been thrown onto the side of the pavement, its belly ripped open to reveal a dark ribbon that looks like a row of pomegranate seeds attached to each other. I run after the car as it turns the corner, shouting at the boy, "You idiot!" I then hear your voices coming from the bedroom window. Another early morning dispute. Even the calm of the early morning is marred by your arguments! It was that silly accident that woke you up. My mother is saying:

—Do you really think you know what's in everybody's best interests? I have told you, my mind is made up, we have to start legal proceedings.

—We will not be starting anything until I've decided.

—What? Am I to remain at the mercy of your laws? Do you really believe that my life is merely an ice cube floating in your drink?

—Listen to me, let us defer this for a while. Let us at least wait until she finishes her baccalaureat exams. Let her at least reach adulthood.

—I no longer care. Let her stay with you if that's what she wants. She can come and visit me when she wants to.

—Calm down and control yourself. I know what I'm saying. Does the poor girl not have enough problems in this house as it is?

—When she grows older, she'll understand our problems and forgive us.

—Why should we blacken her outlook on life at this stage? What right do we have to force an unpleasant reality on her before she has enjoyed even a small amount of happiness?

—Jesus! I really can't understand this happiness that you claim to offer her. She'll soon be a woman; she'll complete her education; then she'll marry and have her children in this torrid heat. That's all there is to it!

—Is that all you have to say? Instead of wishing her a brighter future? It's no wonder that I always see her looking sad and lonely when you reflect your depression onto her in this way.

—My depression? Or that awful mourning ceremony you made us go to that went on for hours without end?

—You've become intolerant. You can no longer bear to perform the most minor social duty. Why are you complaining? Aren't you living the life you want, with all these freedoms you've given yourself? Or has he promised you that he'll marry you?

—Don't be a bastard with me! You're the one who's refusing to give me my freedom. Do you think I'm just a football waiting for you to kick me?

You retaliate:

—For her sake, for the sake of her future only, I'll tolerate these insults. You'll be pleased to know that I've thought long and hard about our situation. I no longer care what you do in your private life, as long as you do no damage to her reputation. I'm the only one who can decide about our divorce. You can do nothing without me, remember that well.

—Ha! The eastern sacrifice for your children! You're talking rubbish. Your life will pass by more quickly than you think. You'll then look back and ask yourself, what have I done in my lifetime?

—I think I'll leave you to make that discovery, my dear.

After a while, I found you in the kitchen making tea. You said, "Good morning" to me, and not another word after that.

We returned to the world of colors the following Friday evening. There was a new atmosphere in the room. Neither one of us wanted to talk about the situation with my mother, or about Millie and David. We embarked on a new cycle with the color red. We discussed its shades and possibilities. I said with a hint of boredom:

—It's Blood Red.

After a little while, I suggested to you:

—Red Thunder.

You nodded your head slowly:

—Possible.

Then you suggested:

—Mysterious Dawn would be better.

—It's more like lipstick, isn't it?

—Yes, do you want to call it Red Lipstick?

—Whatever you like.

I heard a long "Hmmm." It was as though you were fed up. Suddenly you suggested to me:

—Let's move on to this color—I'd call it Wild Reeds.

I continued:

—I'd say it's a Mountaintop Stream.

—That name is too long.

—Then how about Aged Pistachios?

—Yes, it does give that impression.

You then point to another card:

—What about this one, Buttery Yellow?

—Why not Pear, or Ginger.

You reply with a smile:

—Yes, that's pretty, or we could call it Surface of the Marshes.

The night passed as we jumped from one fresh name to another: Shy Lemon, Dream of Jasmine, Rose Petal Water, Nutmeg Flour, Smoked Charcoal, Lovers' Violet, French Vanilla, Buttered Peanuts, Cherry Cola, and Mistaki, Arabic gum.

Suddenly, like a spaceman who's come down to earth, you say to me:

—My daughter, there's something very important you must know about.

—You're getting a divorce?

—No, a war with Iran has started.

4

A Bedouin voice on the radio is singing constantly:

> *"Oh Mother, on my wedding night, sings the cannon,*
>   *dom, dom,*
> *Oh Mother, gunpowder floats, smelling like cardamom,*
>   *dom, dom."*

A few months after full mobilization, our lives are transformed into mere fragments of the lives we had before the war. They soon became a series of days that resembled memories. The events that followed started sliding into each other, like drops of mercury, slowly blending into a gelatinous ball, growing and growing. As the number of military communiqués from the government increases, the misty undulations of the mercury ball become distorted in our dreams, and our days are trapped between two questions: Why, and until when?

The humorous rhymes of my childhood have been replaced by serious patriotic songs:

> *We have marched away,*
> *Marched away to war . . .*

I'm a lover, defending my beloved one,
And we've marched away to war . . .

We sing these anthems during our "volunteering" lessons as we sew cotton bandages that are to be sent off to the front lines, only a few hundred miles to the east. One of the students sings quietly to herself:

My homeland said to me,
I'm your mother
And you are my son . . .
You're the soldier, a bridegroom to be
Your friends will celebrate
And your wedding day will be my day of feasting . . .

She hands me a roll of sticky tape; we have to attach it to the glass in all the windows on both floors, from the inside and the outside. We pray that the air-raid siren won't go off.

I no longer sleep on the roof, and I no longer hear the little birds singing at dawn. Every now and then, we're told not to attend school, on the basis of the instructions issued to the headmistress. The playgrounds are emptied at the sound of a certain bell; or we might be sent home from lessons. We have received full instructions on how to protect ourselves in the event of a bombing raid. We were taught not to hide under the stairways, and to cover our faces with our arms to protect our heads from any possible injuries. In cases of extreme emergency, we have to prostrate ourselves in the street; again we're told to hide our faces as we lie at the edge where the street meets the curb. The first-aid lessons emphasize choking incidents and burns. Several weeks are devoted to providing military training for girls in the Popular Army, the supplementary army corps made up of civilian volunteers.

The general public descended on the food shops in a panic. Everyone started hoarding tinned foods, and any other foodstuffs they could get their hands on. The shops were transformed into empty rooms with puzzled owners: Should they hoard something for their families? Or should they continue saying, "Do not worry, this is a brief crisis, it'll soon pass!" Batteries became scarce, then heating stoves that used petrol and those that burned natural gas, candles, hand-held lanterns, cigarettes, matchboxes, petrol, charcoal, and even refrigerators. My mother kept telling us, "I remember scenes like these during the Second World War." Then she would add calmly, "Of course, I was only a child at the time." A short while later, as if she'd realized what she had just said, she would say, "In spite of that, I still think there is no need to worry." That was until they announced that all travel abroad had been forbidden; then she changed her point of view. That brought back the small gap that separated her feet from the ground. She has started once again moving across the house silently, as though she's gliding rather than walking. She adamantly refuses to let us go to any of the refuge shelters to spend a night or two there with the rest of the people from the neighborhood.

The television programs are presenting brief historical accounts of previous aggressions. Looting, pillaging, towns blockaded, villages and hamlets overrun. We are shown images of galloping stallions and drawn swords, with giant tanks and modern weapons reflected on their surfaces. We're told about the Treaty of Algiers that was signed in 1975 to safeguard national security, maintain the country's unity, and preserve the army. On that basis, Iraq and Iran agreed on Talok's line, which ran down the middle of Shatt al-Arab—the waterway formed by the union of the Tigris and Euphrates Rivers. This was set as the new boundary. In return, each side would withdraw from areas that had been occupied in previous times. It was this agreement that was now being breached.

There were several consecutive days when we were without water, electricity, and telephones. My mother spends hours gazing at her reflection in the large mirror in her bedroom. She takes the alarm clock from her dressing table, placing it in the wooden drawer. A short while later, she takes it out again and buries it underneath her pillow. After another brief interval she heads angrily toward the pillow and extracts it from underneath. She gives it to me, saying, "For God's sake, take this clock to your room, keep it, or throw it out the window. I don't care, just get rid of it—its ticking is driving me crazy!" That day her voice resembled the gobbling of an angry turkey. She was very amused when I told her that the locals called it "Ali Shish" or Fisayfis— "the Smelly Chicken." She said, "Then it's just as well we don't cook it at every feast."

The television news analyst is forever reading the latest reports in his deep, booming voice:

"The agreed international border between Iraq and Iran in the South is Talok's line, the line running down the center of the navigable part of Shatt al-Arab . . ."

My mother has started swinging her leg vigorously in annoyance. She fiddles with her hair, rearranging it time and time again; or she starts chewing some gum, something I know she dislikes intensely. She picks at her thumbnail with the nail of her index finger in a subconscious gesture as she says:

—My God, this heat is awful! Is there no way we can cool ourselves? The juice I've just drunk has started boiling in my stomach. I'll ask your father to get us an electric generator like the one they have at the hospital down the road.

She stops talking for a moment. The heat is stifling her. She opens a white box. It has a green pharmacy icon on its label—a serpent coiled around a cup that it's drinking from. She swallows one of the tablets from the bottle. I ask her:

—What are you taking?

She replies:

—A tranquilizer. By the way, have you heard that all foreigners will be asked to leave the country shortly?

—Not yet. In any case, you're now naturalized. I don't think such a decision would affect you. Does my father know?

She answers me with a look. Then she says:

—I don't care!

—I mean, does he know about the tranquilizers?

She replies nonchalantly:

—I don't care if he does; his sweet powders do not make him a doctor.

She adds:

—There's no point in you telling him tales—it's too late.

She was tired. Dark rings puffed under her eyes. I left her the room and its smothering heat.

I studied by candlelight until the words became ants, roaming across the white page. I felt the heat of those evenings like a newborn baby swaddled in the traditional Arab way, trapped in an unyielding cocoon. It couldn't be unraveled by hand; the only thing that could save me was the return of the electric current. You, father, managed to get hold of a generator, but you donated it to the lab instead of bringing it home. I started losing weight without any effort. My mother gets upset every now and then by what she calls my "skinniness." You try to lighten the mood, saying:

—At least you contributed your excess weight to the war effort, and you've become more beautiful than before.

My mother adds:

—And more dark-skinned than before, because of all that cruel, compulsory military training in the midday sun.

You turn to her:

—Calm down, my dear. War is war—we have to adapt to this situation.

A tranquility has descended upon you. You move around the house distributing droplets of serenity, like the rosewater that is sprinkled about in the mosques. I ask you:

—Baba, will you have to join the Popular Army like all the other men?

You take me in your arms and say:

—My daughter worries about my welfare; I hadn't realized you'd become so slim. What a waist, I can almost get my hands around it. Stop worrying, dearest.

—Baba, don't exaggerate. The mere fact that I now have a waist doesn't make me slim. I wish. Still, I can hardly believe that it was only a few months ago that I was a gigantic blob . . .

You add swiftly:

—One day you'll be a beautiful bride. We just have to be

patient till this temporary crisis passes. And no, I won't have to join the Popular Army, or the Civil Defense or the First-Aid Corps. Those with a heart condition are exempted.

I left the two of you downstairs. The large mirror in my mother's bedroom was calling to me. I stood in front of it, admiring this person with a new figure. How tall and slim she had become. I assumed the first ballet position, and continued through to the fifth. I lifted my hair up so that it fitted with my stance, and admired my profile from both directions. For the first time in my life I was pleased by the reflection I saw before me. I lifted my arms upward; my fingers met. A part of me had become a frame around my face. I tilted my head slightly to the right, and then slightly to the left, like a debutante. I could feel every soft angle of my body. Even my skin color no longer displeased me. I lifted my nose in the air sniffing this calm that had enveloped me. It's mine! I leapt upward performing a low jeté. Then another one, higher, and then a third one, even higher! My body felt as light as my shadow. I attempted a *sauté* with my arms lifted upward again. I repeated the movement time after time with a *changement de pieds*, like a pair of scissors opening and closing. I couldn't believe that I was leaping with total control. I no longer landed with a thud. I could hear what was happening in my joints and in my heels as I bowed to greet the audience and as I bowed to bid them farewell. I tensed, I relaxed, I stretched my body like a cat, I bent forward like an arc; then leaned back like a horizon with my torso extended toward the sky.

The voice of the television presenter haunts me, as though it is reaching me from inside a deep well:

"The two parties to the agreement will form a committee with members from both nations to avoid any source
of conflict as a result of . . ."

The rest of his sentence was swallowed as the electricity
was cut off again.

I palpate my muscles and my bones, my neck and my little breasts. I turn my back to the mirror and admire my
shoulders and my waist. My trunk rises from the center of a
brown apple. Its sides have been drawn tight by a shiny,
sweaty skin. I adopt the pose of the sleeping sea, a quivering
tree, the sun tumbling toward the horizon. I try to remember what I'd been taught in my earliest dance lessons. I perform an encore to the beat of Gypsy drums and the steps of
a Spanish rhapsody. I throw my wings backward as I become the disturbed swan; I control my ankles as they twirl
around each other, accompanying the rhythm of my breathing, with my wrists obeying the sequence of my twirls. My
trunk bends to the side as I touch the tips of my toes, then
stands tall again the way I order it. My suppleness awakes
from its hiding place. Like small dolphins swimming in the
stream, I start to float in the depths of the mirror, in a tunnel of ice and silver.

Suddenly the electric current returns. The television
expresses its point of view like a strange guest who has
awakened, startled, from an unplanned nap on the sofa.

"The next program is the explanation of Article 5. To
safeguard the territorial integrity of both nations, both
parties agree that the land and river borders will not be
infringed and that they are permanent and final."

The deep voice of the presenter reaches me from downstairs, now announcing "Images from the battlefield."

At school, they put up, for the benefit of the students, maps showing the borders with Iran, and images of the border disputes. They explained to us about treaties from the turn of the century, amendments, agreements and additions to the treaties, addendums to the protocols, minutes of the agendas, details involved in mapping out the borders, the meetings, discussions, the ministerial letters. Then the escalation commenced. It started with the breaching of the treaties and all the consequences which followed, leading to the violation of our airspace. We could hear the sounds of the military aircraft as they took off and landed at the old Muthana airport—the old civilian airport in West Baghdad—their sound drowning out the melodies from our musical instruments. The walls of our classroom are covered with slogans and victory banners. Instead of having physical education classes in the morning, we're given additional lectures in political awareness and cultural education, and civil defense instructions.

The dance and music classes weren't banned, but the headmistress read out to us the latest decision regarding the future of the School of Music and Ballet. Funding for overseas postgraduate studies had been discontinued, due to the current situation. One outstanding student from the entire school might be awarded a brief visit abroad as an appreciation of his or her efforts to excel. As for the rest of the students who graduated from the school, they could no longer gain admission to any of the universities to study another subject. The allocated seats at the colleges were withdrawn, and the students had one of two choices. Either to continue studying music or dance, taking it up as a career, or to leave the school and study literary or scientific subjects elsewhere in order to be eligible to go to university after that.

It was in this way that the School of Music and Ballet was classified as superfluous. Many students applied for transfer forms in order to move on to "real" schools. The total number of students in the school was halved. A few studios and classrooms were closed down. Khoshaba, the school janitor with the tufty mustache and wide broom, left the school to look after his wife. Both his sons had been called away for military service. There was chaos at the school as students embarked on their life-altering courses, handing in their musical instruments and dance costumes. Some were justifying their decision to leave. Others, including me, were justifying their decision to stay. We bade farewell to those who were leaving, calling them "traitors"; they turned around as they went through the school gates, calling us "dreamers." I would have become one of the traitors were it not for the arrival of a new dance trainer who'd taken up her appointment just two weeks prior to that. Madame had recently returned from the Soviet Union; she was an Iraqi ballerina in her early thirties who had been trained there. Something about the dark color of her skin made me think twice about my decision to leave with the others, and what she said to me in the corridor after we'd met: "I'll turn you into a butterfly."

I joined her, in spite of your comments, Father, that my enthusiasm would soon be cut down like the ration list, as my activities would be considered "unnecessary" in the present circumstances. The policy of "temporary freezing" had been applied to the flavorings projects as well. It had been put on hold until a future date. Everybody said, "Until the war is over. It will reopen when God wills it."

Madame leaps; I follow with a leap. She freezes; I freeze with her. She loses her temper; I wait for her to calm down. She fumes at the slightest error, or hesitation, or if there is any delay in the start of our training sessions. We don't dare call her anything other than Madame. Outside, the war rages on, divided between the battlefront, the television, and the radio that was always by your ear at home. My mother wonders why the generator you found was taken, as she opens the mail she'd received from England via one of her contacts. Our reflections in the mirrors defy the laws of gravity, but Madame doesn't care that I'm about to pass out in the heat. For her, I'm still on trial.

The conflict with Iran escalated into a full-blown war. Territories and crowded cities were bombarded with heavy artillery. The armed forces gathered at the borders. The call went out for a countrywide mobilization. Shatt al-Arab and the Strait of Hormuz were closed to all navigation.

Madame enrolled me in a strict weekly training schedule. She often said that the pursuit of art had made her endure eight hours of training everyday on pointe, in temperatures below freezing. She then told me to sign up for the summer course. It was for the amateurs who'd failed to turn up on registration day. Her dream to save the school was eventually embodied in a small group of six amateurs. Most of the original students had deserted the classrooms and the dance studios. They left through the main entrance, looking for a better, more practical and realistic future. We stayed behind, trying to overcome our attachment to her. She never ceased scolding us, shouting at us, and demoralizing us in that heat. But there was a magic in the duskiness of her skin and in her voice as she spoke of her dream. Her hopes for the troupe, for after the war, made us stick to her like shadows.

We became acquainted with the events of the battlefield through news bulletins about military clashes that flared up at Zain al-Kaws and Saif Sa'ad. We learned new terms like "usurped territories," "regaining Arab rights," "protecting the homeland," and "repelling the aggression," in a series of new political awareness lessons. Whenever we volunteered for additional dance training, Madame would be harsher with us. Especially when the headmistress told us to abandon our performance of *Swan Lake* and prepare instead for a new ballet which would be called "The Bride of Mendili," in honor of the young bride who lost both her arms on her wedding night as a result of enemy bombardment.

One of Madame's first lectures was about lighting. She stood in the center of the large dance studio. The troupe's members squatted on the floor around her. I sat between Ahmed and Farouk, Sara sat between her twin sisters. She started by saying:

—We all know that light is not emitted from the eye, but that we see objects when light falls upon them, outlining their shapes. Their image is thus created on what is called the retina, which lies at the back of the eye.

She started to pace. The black and white panda printed on her shirt moved about among us. She spoke softly and confidently:

—The retina that we allude to in ballet is the audience. It's among the audience that the movements of your bodies are reflected, in the folds of light and shadow that surround you. In the lights, you will dance with beauty or awkwardness, and in the dark, you will also move with beauty or awkwardness. The secret lies in the movement of your muscles, which you've trained, and in the synchronized movement of the light technician above you. He will be the god that provides you with illumination, and you, my little ones, will dance and create life in a sea of shadows.

Her words were beyond us. Farouk got up and whispered in Sara's ear, "What if there's a power cut?"

Madame interrupted him with a smile:

—Farouk, forget these temporary difficulties we're living through. I'm preparing you for the day when you'll look back on these times and they will be distant memories, just faded recollections of hard training sessions. But we have to exert ourselves to justify our efforts.

A short while later, she added:

—I thank you for sharing my dream with me. Were it not for your attendance, we would not be able to save what can be saved.

Farouk adds:

—That is, if we're not called up into the Army, with all the others who were born in our year.

The thought of the battlefront frightens him. He has decided to stay with the troupe in the hope that he'll be exempted from military service on the assumption that he'll serve the theater when he graduates. He adds in a whisper:

—I could never bear arms. It would be better if they let me dance for my homeland.

· · ·

My mother insists on turning off the television, to enjoy the breeze from the fan without any sound. You mute the set, but the images march on. The explosions continue in silence. Our soldiers advance, and their soldiers are beyond the horizon that divides the screen. The figures run, crawl, roll, throw themselves into ditches filled with water or loops of fire, sheltering behind collapsed walls. We see multitudes of tanks, personnel carriers, rocket launchers, snipers, rifles, and gas masks. We see soldiers in their uniforms, their berets on their heads, their bodies divided in two by their green belts; the upper half is held taut bravely, but the lower half runs in every direction. Army boots don't protect the legs from landmines. Men in khaki fight other men in khaki; dead bodies start to fall all around us.

Madame turns around, aware of the beauty of her profile that turns with her in the mirror. She begins her instructions by saying "Please" in Russian:

—*Pojalosta*, when we talk about dance, don't forget the difference between the artist and the dance-hall girl—which is what some people called me when I returned from the snow-covered lands. I left the Soviet Union because the financial support by the Iraqi government was cut off as a result of the war the year before I graduated. I was forced to come home on the first available flight, as I didn't have the means to continue my studies. So I became a "dancer without a degree," and that makes my artistic life even more difficult as I try to establish myself here in the East. There, they called me "The Dark One from the Siberia Institute." They granted me a symbolic degree just before I left. The headmistress at the institute bade me farewell, throwing two snowballs at my back when I left. They all wished me good luck and a speedy return.

She sighed, then continued:

—How ridiculous! Don't think the road is easy. If you're going to abandon it halfway, it would be better if you declare that now.

Nobody declared anything. We remained seated on the ground. The twins exchanged pale glances, as if they had no eyelashes, like a pair of goldfish.

We've started getting used to the images of military maneuvers, shelling, unexpected military communiqués, and the expected ones, which always started, "In the name of God, the Compassionate, the Merciful," and ended with "And may the wicked be shamed." We were bombarded with patriotic songs, the National Anthem, verses from the Koran, and the slogan that the martyrs were the most generous of all. These colors started to fade. Civilian life began to resemble a khaki chameleon, which pricked up its ears at the sound of the air-raid siren, wandering quietly through the darkened streets, until the curfew is imposed.

Madame's lectures descended on us like pouring rain. She embarked on the laws of physics, telling us that our bodies' stability depended on static balance, kinetic balance, and leverage points. She dissected each one of us, demonstrating to the others our strengths and weaknesses. We spent many hours training, and at her insistence we left the word "shame" at the door when we entered her class.

—I want you to understand each other's bodies well, because we are all one group. That means that we'll move as one body. Embarrassment and shame can't dance together. We must overcome the physicality of our bodies. That's the art of ballet.

When she shouts at us, "Is that understood?" our breath has been scattered to the corners of the studio—no one has the strength to answer.

—Dance is logic; the movements of the body are logical. Your presence here is logical. Synchronicity is the essence we must find before we introduce the element of music.

We glance at the hired pianist, who awaits her instructions, puzzled and in a quandary. We all knew that he had a pierced nostril; maybe he was hoping to escape the Army.

—The synchronicity between the movement of the arms, the legs, and the face is the backbone of each and every step. Concentrate on planning before the movement. Don't think of the impression you will create onstage. You should rather be listening to the way your joints bend. Allow them to determine how you can reach into yourselves rather than just running around in those thick stockings that reveal the contours of your bodies to the audience. And now, I want the girls to climb the boys' bodies like ivy. Ahmed opened his arms wide to receive Sara, allowing his big white teeth to speak on his behalf,

—Come on, Soosoo, cling to me like ivy.

The shelling of the town of Mendili was followed by the shelling of the city of Khanaqin, and the town of Zurbatia, less than an hour's drive away, and the petrochemical works in Nafut Khana and Basra. The military communiqué that day announced:

"Our brave forces have surprised the enemy soldiers and inflicted upon them heavy losses, including the destruction of eleven tanks, twenty-four vehicles, four bulldozers, one personnel carrier, and one helicopter. The enemy shelling ended in failure, leaving behind them columns of smoke and flame of fire as a result of the violent clashes."

The only thing that separated us from the outside world were the giant mirrors reflecting our images back to us. A wooden barre encircled the room along the mirrors. It surrounded us like a rope, held in position by steel handles; it supported us as we performed our training exercises. That wooden support hid our flaws, and Madame was always shouting:

Pojalosta, get away from that barre!

She taught us how to take off rather than to leap. She would make us imagine virtual rivers that we had to fly across, and rainbows we had to pass beneath, with our noses held high in the air. She made us flow out through our hands as she asserted that sliding differed from walking. During the hours when she trained the girls on pointe, she would scream at us to stop eating fattening foods. She told us to stuff our shoes well with cotton wool, to protect our toes from injuries. How many times she shouted at us:

—You are girls made of wood! I will enter you in a competition to find the best Coppelia. You're all rigid; for God's sake, move faster!

For her, everything had a rule, a schedule, and very accurate timing.

We found it extremely difficult to achieve her dream. Ahmed turned up late for class, wearing his open leather

Bata slippers, to keep his feet cool. His attitude was that he was doing Madame a favor by attending the training sessions in the time he had left before he was called up to the Army. He came in saying:

—I'm sorry, everybody, to have held you up. I've been using my car as a taxi, and my last fare took me to the other side of town.

He enters coolly into the boys' changing rooms. Madame waits for him to emerge by the door. He comes out, a large bulky body wearing training shorts. She strikes him on the chest, saying:

—And who do you think you are—Spartacus? This is your last warning for being late. If your punctuality fails to improve, we'll soon cut down the number of members in the group!

He smiles back at her. He knows very well that she can't replace him and Farouk. The young men are all at the battlefront, the young girls are getting married, and all the other students were not about to come back after having been accepted in their new schools. Since Ahmed had started using his car as a taxi during his spare time, he'd become our main source of local news: the price of tomatoes, the daring raids in the front lines, the victory celebrations, the results from enemy bombardment, the latest directives from the passport office, the activities organized by the Ministry of Culture and Information, the latest books that had been translated into Arabic, the deportation of Iranians and their replacement with Egyptian laborers, the latest joke from *Alef Ba* magazine, and on one occasion he brought us shell fragments from the last missile that had landed on Baghdad.

The weeks that passed seemed very long. During that

time, edicts were issued classifying the priorities of civilian life, separating essential consumer items from nonessential ones. It was at this time that all travel abroad was banned except for businessmen, patients seeking treatment and their companions, and those residing outside Iraq. Activity in the foreign embassies diminished; then their employees started returning to their home countries, leaving behind two soldiers to guard the building and a checkpoint. Some of them entrusted a nearby embassy to look after their affairs. The number of foreigners and guest lecturers at the universities dwindled, especially when the air raids intensified. Some sites on the outskirts of Baghdad were damaged. Houses were hit in Karrada, Zayoona, and Mansour, the affluent suburbs of the city of Baghdad. We became especially concerned when we looked out of our classroom window and saw an antiaircraft battery mounted in Zawra Park, next to the Lovers' Fountain.

Madame draws herself up. She stands like a ruler, yet she's made of thick brown rubber tendons. She bends and stretches her body with the greatest of ease, as though the bones in her body are not human. She says:

—The French believe that perfection can be attained only in death. Ballet seeks perfection, so you have to push yourselves in your training close to death, without succumbing to it, as that would end the performance.

We didn't know which performance she was talking about. It was as though we were all awaiting her secret instructions to undertake a military mission from which we might or might not return. In spite of that, we found a new meaning in each lesson: the music, the steps, the five positions, the expressions of happiness, sorrow, fear, revenge, daring, comedy, and determination in the choreography and its narrative. She took us into the world of endurance. We swore at the end of every lesson that we'd never return, especially when she stopped us from drinking any water during the breaks in training. During the warm-up that preceded each training session, the one who arrived before the others at the barre would ask himself if the others were going to turn up. Even Farouk, who was sometimes late, because he had to stop and wait in a queue to buy eggs for his family, would eventually show up.

Another military communiqué:

> "Our Armed Forces have successfully erected a bridge across the Karoun River. They have crossed to the other bank, cut off all communication between Abadan and Sheikh Ibdair and tightened their siege of Abadan. The Karoun River extends from northern Iran and flows into Shatt al-Arab at the city of Mohamara. Its width ranges from four hundred to six hundred meters, and it passes through open fields and cultivated orchards. The crossing of this river is the first crossing of a major waterway by our brave forces."

She takes us into the world of rhythm. She shouts, "Tempo, my troupe, tempo," demonstrating to smooth music, saying "Legato," then jumping into discordant notes, saying "Staccato." She is able to move her joints with amazing professionalism. She has complete control over her musculature, full flexibility in her trunk, and a piercing look. Her elegance is stunning as she turns her profile at a right angle to her movements. Her vitality as she performs a battement tendu or a pirouette regenerates with every spin. Her porte de bras makes her a queen on pointe as she explains an adagio. She dances as though she has unburdened herself of the weight of her body with her first step. It was thus that she spoke to us of freedom as she danced; she spoke to us of flowers made of feathers sliding across a silver bowl. Her wrists twirl in harmony with her ankles and hips and the way she holds her head. She contemplates the simplicity of the movement or its complexity, its length or its brevity, the rigidity or laxity required, how far to stretch or tense in an atmosphere of black and white, or in the colors that reflect her mood. When she dances, we know that she is breaking free.

My life consists of no more than my attempts to graduate academically, plus attending the dance sessions three times a week to train with Madame's troupe. At four o'clock I meet Sara at the stairs leading to the entrance; the gateway forms a frame around her. She is so thin, as if she's a survivor from a famine. Her delicate bones protrude from underneath her pale skin. Her voice is so soft it can barely be heard. She's like a hollow sugar cane when the wind blows through it, whistling gently. Her twin sisters follow behind her. They compete with her in their pallor and skinniness, like a pair of flattened fish. Their thin legs are almost rickety. Farouk jokingly says, "The two matchsticks have arrived." Their eyes, in spite of the high eyebrows arching upward, are free of all expression. Their eyelids hesitate as they close, like dangling stage curtains that have been left half-open. Sara and her two sisters resemble Pinocchio in triplicate. They come down the stairs like puppets, moved along by their strings. I was told that their mother was French, and that she looked like Olive Oyl, Popeye's girl-friend. Farouk likes to tease them to see how they respond. Sometimes he'd ask them where they hid their fins, or if they sweat like the rest of the human race. If the three sisters stood in a straight line, all I could see from the side would be a column of hair, curled in the shape of blond buns. Their feet are turned out in preparation for the first movement of the dance.

Another military communiqué has been issued:

"One of our brigades has established itself on the near bank of the Karoun River. A division of infantry crossed the river using boats and other watercraft. The engineering corps advanced with them to improve the crossing points and facilitate the crossing by the tanks, personnel carriers, and other vehicles."

Ahmed comes in wearing his usual leather Bata slippers. His car keys are dangling from his pocket. Hanging from his key is a little white cat he named Lucky Fluffy. He calls out to Farouk, taking him away to introduce him to his new girlfriend, who's waiting in the car. Farouk follows him eagerly to meet this stout girl who fills up the entire front seat of the car. When they return to the dance studio, Farouk asks, "Couldn't you find someone fatter than that? What do they feed her all day? Yeast?" Ahmed laughs out loud. His teeth reply, "Don't you see that we've had enough of girls who look like dried reeds?" He then whispers, "Round Face is here," and we know that Madame has finally arrived.

We embark on the classics, exhausted, on tiptoe. We listen to Chopin and excerpts from Rachmaninoff. She explains Bach's fugue. We wipe the ground with our bodies in a modern dance piece. The music of Jean Michel Jarre descends upon us from the large speakers in the corners of the studio. The notes drip down from their pores like drops of water that don't wet us. She says:

—Always remember that you are never taught anything unnecessarily.

After a while she adds:

—Not in this studio, nor outside it.

She turns toward Farouk, who thought she'd not been looking his way as he shook his shoulders gracefully at one of the twins, the one who was ten minutes older. She says:

—Farouk, please try to leave your origins in folkloric dancing behind you. You're now studying ballet.

The official government price lists change daily, along with the television announcers. Most of them are now women. The young men of military age have all joined the Army. The older, white-haired announcer reads the military communiqués in his deep, booming voice. His latest announcements are about economic necessities. Black banners now hang outside homes and mosques announcing the death of the martyred soldiers in big white letters. Tents have been erected in the streets for the men's mourning ceremonies, and the roads are closed from both ends for three days. Shots are fired into the air from a private handgun; a martyr's mother ululates. The wife of a soldier missing in no-man's-land swears that she will not cut her son's hair until his father returns safely. The members of the Popular

Army patrol the streets when darkness falls, and the soldiers on leave insist that civilian life is no longer what it used to be. We're warned not to sit near windows or to sleep upstairs. We're advised not to use too many candles for lighting, nor to use the rooftops, or to go out into the garden with a lit cigarette during an air raid, even if it's only a military exercise.

Farouk's rough manners and his salty, colored skin take me back relentlessly to a dusty track. Its shadows swim toward me from the road leading to the mud houses by the riverbank. He tells me during our break of his extended family, who live in the rural areas around the Diyala River. His uncle worked at a little shop outside the School of Folkloric Dance, and that was how he ended up here. I feel instinctively the special friendship that awaits us. Madame's voice returns to us:

—My little ones, do not concentrate when you're in front of the mirror on only one of your limbs, forgetting the rest of your body, allowing it to flap around foolishly. Embrace the body you see standing in front of you, frame it, correct its errors starting from the feet and the trunk—they are your centers of gravity. You have to differentiate between the weight-bearing leg and the resting leg. Release your joints; they are the key to the beauty we seek to achieve. It's the marriage of the mechanics of the materials, our bodies, and the transparency of the soul, the music. The shoulders are there for the doves to perch on. It's a concerto of union, the merger of sound and movement. Don't forget the crown to all these elements—expression. Stop dancing like kittens and walking like the March of the Fools. Show me feelings, emotions. What is wrong with you? Even dolphins can express themselves!

From the eastern borders we receive the news of the war. The battles have intensified on the front lines, and we have adapted to their consequences on the rear lines. Most of the women are now wearing black. Social introductions are now based on the fact that this woman is the sister of a martyr; that one is the mother of a martyr, or the fiancée of a soldier missing in action; and this child is the daughter of a prisoner of war. The files of the students studying abroad have been closed. Scholarships overseas have ceased and the checks are no longer being sent out. A large number of the students came back to take up their positions on the front lines. The number of buses bringing back the corpses of the martyrs to their families' homes has increased. It's a sad trip in a little bus for the mother holding her son's beret. She wails from the back window as it stops at the traffic lights. She insists that this is her dead son's wedding day. We have become accustomed to death and its tales. The television ruminates on the enemy's losses and ours.

We persevered in the dance studio for three long years. Madame was never content with us, in spite of our efforts to improve our performance according to her instructions regarding training, slimming, and leaving embarrassment behind us. She asked for the impossible. The tips of our toes could no longer bear it. She dragged us with her to a world we felt was melting in the choking heat. We were all waiting for the end of the war, as though what she called the final performance would be on that day of salvation. She pointed without hesitation to our shortcomings. Dance had become a personal debt we had to pay her. Sometimes she would lash out at us without any forewarning:

—You want to hear the applause, don't you? Have you fallen into the fame seeker's trap? How naïve! Didn't I tell you that all the seats behind the curtains might be filled with sea lions who will applaud you from all directions? I promise you that; but I can't promise to get you through the agonies of this art. We must work harder and harder!

She enters in a suicidal mood. She shows a clipping from a newspaper that described us cynically as a group of saviors of culture. She poured out her anger onto us, saying:

—No one gives us any credit, and that is all our fault. How easy it is for a misprint to convert us from a dance group into a dunce group!

Farouk objected:

—Madame, it's nobody's fault. We put in all this effort to please you, and in an attempt to understand this road that we were set on since we were children. Maybe they did us wrong when they exposed us to this world that has made us fear what they call "real life." We know nothing but dance, and that language is useless in this time of war. Maybe we made a mistake when we clung to what you call "the dream." Maybe the time has come for us to break this bond, if it's going to turn us into nervous wrecks in this way. Anyway, the chances of the war ending soon are minimal. We're about to graduate and leave; we should be wise and not ask for the impossible.

He stopped speaking for a few moments to regain his breath, his words crowding his thoughts. He lifted his hands upward:

—First of all, Ahmed is going to marry his girlfriend. Second, I will have to join one of the military units, and all our efforts will be wasted. Madame, we've become attached to you in spite of the way you shout at us and your constant bad temper. We appreciate what you're doing for us, but for God's sake, try and understand our point of view as well. Do you really think you can obtain the revenge for your misfortune through us? Why do you use us like puppets, to prove that your studies with the Russians were not wasted? At least you had a chance to see the real world. What about us? We're about to exchange ballet training for training with bullets!

Farouk exploded in her face, red with emotion. He then apologized and started to leave the hall. As he was about to kick the door open, he turned around again, saying angrily:

—And in all honesty . . . it's not the bourgeois applause that you hear in your ears that attracts me to this group, but the pitifully small financial assistance I get for coming here. It's for that that I exhaust myself in training, in order to be able to feed my little brother.

After his outburst, all we could hear was the sound of our breathing. It was as though we were all facing the mistiness of the coming days. The news from the battlefront was vague. New age groups were being called up for military service, and the Popular Army troops were sent into battle. Madame sat down on one of the chairs nearby. She lit a cigarette nervously, saying in a desperate voice:

—My God, my children are maturing faster than their muscles. This cannot be. *Pojalosta*, when will this nightmare end?

Whenever she said *pojalosta* in that tone, it was as though she were calling up her guardian angel.

· · ·

We became accustomed to the sound of the air-raid siren. The children in the street started imitating it to perfection. Sometimes we were unable to differentiate the sound of the children playing from the real thing. Because of the petrol crisis, cars with even-numbered plates had to use the road on one day, and those with odd-numbered plates the next. Natural gas was distributed by coupons. At first, the man who sold the canisters would drive past the houses frequently, blowing his annoying horn; now he's nowhere to be seen. The streets are full of Volkswagen cars, assembled in Brazil. There are so many of them, the people have started calling them stray dogs. They hang around the petrol stations looking for gas canisters and petrol. On the main roads leaving the city, there are people standing with cans of paint and brushes, to paint out the lights of the passing cars and cut down their glare. Our lives shut down when darkness descends. I climb stealthily to the rooftop. There I spend stolen moments, watching the flame of Al-Dora refinery in the distance.

While the shelling continued, we were able to present only a few uninspiring performances. We repeated them at the National Theater, at the Stage and Cinema Auditorium, and at Al-Mansour Cinema in the Celebrations Arena. We got fed up with the repetition of it all, with Ahmed's performance as Sindbad, and Farouk's as the emperor of China in an excerpt from *The Great Wall*. Sara was an emerald, I was a diamond, and the twins appeared as rubies in *The Basket of Jewels*. We would then end with a waltz by Strauss. We had one final chance before we graduated—the Babylon Festival. The light of challenge returned to Madame's eyes. She talked of a modern dance work that would start with eggs hatching on stage to reveal the first creation. She wanted to produce Adam from one of Eve's ribs to the strains of classical music interspersed with snatches of sorrowful jazz. We trained every day. She spoke with excitement of our chance to appear in front of foreign ensembles. She then decided that we would also present a work she called *Funeral of an Artist,* insisting that it was her life's story and that she would retire immediately after the performance, saying, "Anyway, an Indian fortune-teller once told me I would die at the age of thirty-five."

It was a crazy time. When she showed us the steps and movements of the final death scene, it was as though she died each time she danced for us. She twirled around herself with the most graceful of movements, as though she were drilling the floorboards beneath her feet with her agonized twisting. She concentrated all that she had taught us into that sequence, so that we could perform it on her behalf. In the space of a few minutes, we would fall, like flies, in front of the foreign delegates whom she described as "a flock of penguins." She went on: "They wear their black evening suits, and come here to criticize our performance. Don't let their civilized appearance distract your feet from their role." Sara trembled like an autumn leaf from the moment the first note was played, and Farouk developed violent abdominal cramps during the breaks.

Our performance was a success; it combined modern dance of the creation with the classicism of the artist's funeral and the legend of Ishtar. We experienced the terror of expressing ourselves for the first time at the Babylon Festival, in front of the rows of curious eyes scattered around the seats of the stone amphitheater. But in spite of that success, in the end we felt that the torture we had endured with this creature would not take us beyond the last stop, the train station where we'd gotten off. We had presented a comprehensive performance, but we left it behind amid the ruins of Babylon, to swelter in the August heat.

Military communiqué:

> "The enemy has used heavy artillery and military aircraft to shell civilian areas, economic targets, and trading vessels as they entered and left Shatt al-Arab. In the latest battles to the east of Basra, the total enemy losses were sixty-five hundred dead. Eleven warplanes were downed and twenty armed personnel carriers were destroyed. Our forces also seized a large number of heavy guns and rifles, all in working order. Our losses were six hundred five martyrs, eighty-one tanks, and a hundred three personnel carriers."

Another year passes by. Then, finally, we are forced to give up. The school has closed its doors to both professionals and amateurs. Our troupe was the last serious group of students who graduated on pointe. The drums of war were still beating. As we exited through the school gate, Madame smoked a cigarette in desperation and said:

—We're like a group of beavers; we gnaw each other's dreams to build ourselves nests over waters, not realizing the waters are already stagnant.

We soon heard that Farouk had become a cook in one of the infantry divisions that were training in the city of Hilla.

Ahmed used his taxi to take soldiers to their collection points near the front lines, and brought those on leave back to Baghdad. He had deferred getting married to his fat girlfriend till after the war. That was when Madame advised me to apply to one of the newly set up private colleges. For a fee, they'd opened their doors to the students who'd failed to gain access to Baghdad University and Mustansiriya University. Their fees were what you, Father, called "an arrogant charge." But finally, at Madame's insistence, you agreed. Her visits to our house had become more numerous. You said to her:

—So, in the end, my daughter is to be educated in the private sector!

She answered with an imploring look in her eyes. Out of politeness she addressed you as an older male acquaintance, saying:

—Uncle, I had no father to give me advice; he left me when I was very young. It's my fault that she joined the ballet troupe. I was someone who dreamed, I brought my fantasies with me. I attempted to achieve them through my students. How wrong I was; it seems that the heat and the war will not end. I feel responsible that she's been left in midstream, she hasn't become a dancer, and she will not have specialized in any field, unless she enrolls in one of these colleges. I beg you; I don't want to see my life's scenario being repeated a second time.

You sat down between the two of us; then you sighed a little and said:

—I objected to this choice of school from the start; she wouldn't be there if it weren't for her mother. But what has happened has happened, and I should thank God that I'm not awaiting the return of a son from the battlefield. God has his wisdom.

You said it as though you were forgiving us our dream.

I chose to study English literature at the new, private "Heritage College." The boredom of the lectures was unbearable. The fear of the front lines made the students play a game of musical chairs with fate. I was there for two years, until that day you became unwell, on the road from Baghdad to Zafraniya. I came back from college that day to find my mother eerily quiet. The driver was crying, and Madame was there, waiting for me. Abu Nidhal's widow and their colored woman servant, Heyla-Um al-Abid, were there, too, preparing coffee for everyone. Madame and all these other people, here in our house? Who contacted them? Why are they here? They were all in a state of shock.

Your heart had stopped beating.

How can this sudden hush occur without any warning! Didn't you know that I don't like these kinds of surprises? Why didn't you prepare me for this yesterday, for example? Your face, covered in that white shroud, had a faint smell of caramel—something that my mother no doubt hadn't noticed, lost in her cloud of smoke. Yes, I don't like surprises. But how could I have prepared myself for something like this? How can any girl prepare herself for this moment . . . I'm sitting in your lap now. It's Friday. You whisper in my ear, telling me to stop fidgeting and squirming. You do your best to make me listen to the verses of the Koran being read aloud on television. You tell me that the first thing I must learn is to listen with respect to these calm verses, as you hold me tightly in your lap with your long arms.

But what's happening now? Everything has stopped. I can no longer hear my mother's clock ticking in my ear. The years of dancing have ended, leaving only the battered pink silk toe shoes that I have hung by my bed as a souvenir. Khaddouja has gone; you must stay! Someone behind me mentions the washrooms. I don't know how long they allowed me to gaze at you, then a hand pulled me away. I touched your cold lax face as they took your body off to be washed—the final act before burial. Everything around me is turning into a corpse.

I dragged my feet after that to complete my final two years. I recall the scenes of your passing every time I stand in front of the mirror remembering my braid. My relationship with Madame became a deep friendship, with a strange feeling of sympathy. I don't want to disturb my mother. She takes her pills to calm herself down even further. She's like a tortoise as she moves from one spot to another. She still awaits the mail from England. My days at college have become an unbearable drudgery. Maybe I was only doing it for your sake. I had no difficulty getting through the academic year with minimal concentration.

Finally the loose financial and legal ends involving your project have been tied up. I spent several sessions with your lawyers and accountants, signing papers and documents on behalf of my mother. After that came the day we burned all that you left behind: samples, boxes, chests, containers, flavorings, colors, paints, scents, and lab mixtures. The gardener helped us pile them up in the middle of the garden. He carefully set them alight. The colored fumes crackled and blended into rich clouds that gathered underneath the leaves of the orange trees. My mother retreated to watch them from behind the glass of the kitchen window. She stayed inside, gazing out in a drugged haze. Her blank stare pierced the purple smoke, then settled into it.

The burial rites; the prayers for the dead; reading the entire Koran: I lived through a period of such depression, I felt as if I was weighed down by the heavy air I held in my hands.

5

The war has been dragging its heavy feet from the day the first military communiqué was issued. The ages of those called up for compulsory military services have been extended to both younger boys and older men. Calls have gone out for more voluntary contributions. Laws forbidding travel abroad have become more numerous and varied. Foreign magazines have disappeared from the shelves in bookshops. Imported goods have been replaced by local produce. Pharmacies have been banned from selling contraceptive pills in an effort to increase the population and replace the losses at the battlefields. The television natters with promotions encouraging marriage and early conception. In a new trend called "mass weddings," large halls are hired out, complete with all varieties of foods and sweets. Couples are married there en masse. Each couple takes their turn at cutting the gigantic white cake, using a knife decorated with colored ribbons.

Photographers cover these group weddings eagerly, swarming among the guests like flies. The papers announce special offers at the main hotels: Al-Rasheed, Al-Mansour Melia, Ishtar-Sheraton, Palestine Meridien, and Al-Sadeer Novotel. Ads for "Wedding Island" encourage newlyweds to spend their honeymoons there, accompanied by price reductions at the Rainbow Company, which specializes in the embroidery of wedding dresses. Other promotions include special prices for hair styling at Rumoush, Suad, and Asmahan's Hair Salon for women. A fortune-teller offers to predict the names of university graduates who would make suitable marriage partners. Financial grants for early marriage are handed out by the accounts office at the College of Tourism at Mustansiriya University.

Violent clashes continue at the battlefront in both the central and southern sectors. The war has been transformed from a war of lightning attacks into a static war involving dugouts and trenches. We've started hearing details of the battles on the eastern banks of the Karoun River and around Abadan. Massive amounts of military equipment were abandoned on the battlefields. In the vicinity of Deyzfoul and Al-Shosh, and in the third major battle for the town of Al-Khafajia, there were thousands killed. Mines have now been sown, adding a new dimension to the war as they rip up the soldiers' bodies, turning the earth underfoot to burning flames. The bridges across the Karoun River have sustained heavy damage, and the blockade of the cities continues in an atmosphere of sacrifice that is claiming human lives in unprecedented numbers.

The last I heard, Farouk had been wounded in the battles of West Gaylan. Ahmed disappeared; we lost all contact with him after the battle of Besayteen. Sara got a job at the Iraqi Fashion House, at the intersection of Maysaloon Street and Al-Rubaiee Road. When their shows ceased as a result of the economic restrictions, she joined her twin sisters. The older twin was working as a seamstress. She sewed shiny new buttons on the dresses displayed at the folkloric fashion shows, replacing old faded ones that had lost their sparkle. The younger twin had perfected the art of darning. She spent her days patching and repairing the traditional costumes, awaiting the day they would go on display again.

The telephone rings! It's Madame on the line. She's in the vicinity and invites me to come with her on a visit to a group of her friends. She laughingly calls them "the group from the defunct regime"—supporters of the monarchy in Iraq, which was overthrown in a coup in 1958. A few minutes later she picks me up in her car. I'd changed in a rush. She chats about the new performance that has been suggested to her, and about my chance to meet some of the new, "fresh faces."

We reach her artist friend's flat. He opens the door—a round face with a Greek nose. Underneath his small nostrils is a blond mustache that sets off the color of his eyes. When he smiles hello, his eyes are hidden by his droopy eyelids. He takes Madame in his arms; in his glass two centimeters of red wine are trembling. When the gasps of joy at their reunion have quieted down, I'm introduced to the four friends . . . he is a sculptor with a little belly that has started to grow with the late night. Then there's a dancer with taut muscles, and a female architect with a strand of gray hair behind her ear. There was also a stage actor with a cigarette lit from the embers of the previous one. The narrow entrance leads to a spacious area where turquoise-colored cushions are piled high. They lean against some henna-colored ones that encircle a low coffee table, which is large enough to accommodate six people around it. The evening starts with reminiscences unfamiliar to me, floating with the smoke amid the quivering candlelight.

An hour of generalized conversation follows: hopes for the war to end, fluctuations in the price of foodstuffs and medicines, lack of building materials, how to maintain an artistic output when the private galleries and painting exhibitions have closed down, the lack of prizes for new artistic works and stage productions, the scarcity of glossy paper for magazines and ordinary paper for books and other publications. Madame has become involved in lengthy discussions with her actor friend; they're using French and Russian terms in their conversation. The woman architect interrupts them with a drunken laugh: "Ha! Have you started cursing each other?" It was a classic cliché that didn't go down well in the simple, friendly atmosphere of the gathering. She annoyed me with her attempts to display her new set of porcelain white teeth. They must have cost her a sizable amount of money in the present circumstances. When they all became engrossed, each one grumbling about their favorite topic, I slid quietly away toward the studio, through the opening where the two rooms met.

I parted the curtain. The quivering cane beads behind me made a clicking noise as they came together again. I've entered a room of moderate size and lighting. Slumbering vapors envelop a distinctive darkness. Scattered structures are illuminated by a multitude of burning candles. The sculptures are placed in a random fashion on the metal shelves fixed to the wall on the left. On the right are several wooden structures of varying heights and sizes, fixed firmly to the floor. Parallel to the shelves is a large wooden table that has been placed in the center of the room. Out of the corner of my eye, I glimpse an open box of long white candles lying by the curtain. I take one and steal a flame for it from a nearby candle that is dying. I start making my way among the works our host has created. I glance stealthily through the open side door, which leads to a small bedroom, furnished with a modern-style bed, a handmade desk, and a ceiling of mirrors.

I reflected on yesterday's events, the battles of Deyzfoul and Al-Shosh. The enemy had gathered large numbers of troops and equipment in the area. Fifteen battalions had been deployed, in addition to large numbers of Revolutionary Guards and volunteers. A total of 700 tanks and 15,000 men were thrown into the battles along a front that extended for over 150 kilometers. The conflicts had raged for several days, but I no longer recall the losses that resulted.

The first work is a life-size sculpture of a newborn baby. His umbilical cord extends from his abdomen to a placenta in the shape of a combat helmet. The second sculpture is of a woman breast-feeding her baby. A pair of khaki helmets protrude from her chest wall where her breasts should be. The third work is the side view of a man kneeling in prayer, submitting himself with resignation. On the table farther away are some smaller sculptures: a donkey in evening dress, a mouse cracking a whip, a sow breast feeding a man, a cat copulating with a dog. A deer's head with angry eyes hangs down from the wall, along with an African mask made of dark wood and yellowed straw. They both seem to be looking at the metal shelf, where a hand made of white gypsum is trying to crawl. Some of the works are covered with the dust of neglect. Two hands are greeting each other.

One hand is supplicating, another is clenched in a mysterious way. There's a hand rebelling, another is relaxed, another one makes a victory sign. There's a hand bleeding, and another one is begging. A hand is pensive, another is playing, one is weary of waiting. There's a small sign that says STUDIES; beside it is an outstretched hand overflowing with kindness.

There's a statue called *Routine.* It's a man trying to get out of a pyramid through its smooth sides; he wears it like a dress, glazed with two hands emerging from its sides and two feet emerging from its base. The head emerges from the apex; the feet sink into the gypsum base as if he's being pushed down by the heavy weight he's bearing. One of the sides gives the impression that his stance is unstable, while the other angle gives the impression that he's swaying but still in control. It's the view from the back that reveals how hampered he is, with his hands being trapped in this three-dimensional pyramid that he's trying so hard to get rid of. The three corners are flat and repetitive, the straight lines are sharp, but the expression on his face remains the same regardless of the viewer's position. Beside him is a brown eagle whose wings bear an image of the Virgin; behind this is a modern sculpture depicting a number of horses' heads that look like upright hammers. One of the pieces is a large combat helmet that has become a cradle for a baby with no facial features. He's being rocked by a hand cloaked in subtle darkness. Two copper doves are nailed to the wall by their wings with rusty pins. In front of them is the outline of a dried tree with irregular measurements, decorated with Japanese lettering.

The reports of the military analysts circulate among the

works of art, disembodied voices swirling around in the ether:

> "Waves of men flowed down onto the battlefield. Our forces repelled the attack by these infinite hordes, preventing the enemy from achieving his dream in reaching the borders. They were attempting to create a breach in the front over a small distance. To this end they gathered in exceptionally large numbers. Our forces in that area, the Al-Sheeb Pass, which is only eleven kilometers wide, remain steadfast and brave."

On a colored traditional rug is a miniature copy of one of Michelangelo's works. It's the congested face of a fat bald man with his mouth pouting out. He's blowing out, with his lips forming a circle and his eyebrows lifted upward as high as possible, looking like a fountain in an Italian palace. On another stand is a smooth wooden sculpture, part male and part female. It sits pondering its ambiguous position. There's a glass tank with dried cockroaches in it. There are some thin, long, indistinct masses with no title. They look like the limbs of a plant dreamed up by Giacometti; they're bowing to larger masses lined up behind them like a military unit commanded by Henry Moore. I see embroidered toys in the shape of a fish or a flower made by the soldiers during their long periods on duty. There's a sketch in charcoal of a woman wearing an abaya. She's washing her feet in the waters of a calm river. Her mouth gapes slightly on one side as though a hand has secretly stolen her smile away. A snake is shedding its khaki skin beside a drawing in black and white, of a pretty girl with hairy legs, and a photo of a huge glass structure being eaten by giant cracks that look like shredded spiders' webs.

The curtain behind me is clicking again. He enters, looking for an ashtray, smiling gently:

—It's not an exhibition, as you can see. This is my abandoned workshop.

He bends forward, putting his hands together, making a mock Indian salute, adding:

—I present to you, dear miss, the retired sculptor.

He moves on, fidgeting.

—On the contrary, the sculptures express what is happening outside.

—Yes, and the outside is killing what is inside me. What you see around you has been sitting on these shelves for several years now. Do you smoke?

—No, thank you. Is your mustache naturally blond, or is it the nicotine?

He laughs, replying:

—I'm blond, from my head down to my feet.

He then adds:

—I envy you. I've tried on many occasions to give up this addiction, especially when I abandoned the studio.

—Do you mean you're no longer sculpting?

He doesn't reply. He continues to hunt for an ashtray.

—Why don't you try chewing gum instead of smoking?

He smiles:

—Can you imagine what I'd look like walking through the gates of the military base chewing gum? Just imagine it, ha!

He adds:

—We're about to finish the second bottle of wine. Won't

you join us? Madame is translating a poem for us about a flock of birds who have all had one wing cut off, so they all have to help each other to fly. The horizon is filled with pairs of birds hugging each other on one side, and flapping their one wing on the other side in order to soar together. Apollinaire, I think.

He starts to smoke. He can't remain still. He looks again at his sculptures as if he's seeing them for the first time. He says:

—Do you think people would help each other more if each person lost a hand or an arm?

—Isn't that what's happening, one way or another?

—So you think that we'll have peace again soon? Hmm . . .

He sank into a cloud of silence, but in spite of his silence, all his body parts remained in constant motion. I couldn't make up my mind if his honey-colored eyes were attractive or not. It was those droopy eyelids that left me undecided, but I was sure the eyes were incisive and deep. His hands were swollen, and his leg—it never stopped shaking.

A review of the month's news items interferes with our first meeting.

"A number of our military units in the region of Al-Khafajia have been redeployed. This repositioning was undertaken to increase the troops' security and strengthen their positions. The enemy played no role in these maneuvers."

I interrupt his daydreams:

—Your works are varied and expressive. Did you start sculpting at an early age?

—Our meeting doesn't have to be this formal, you know. It's true that I won't ask you to dance with me straight-away, but, my little one, if you allow me to call you that . . .

He carries on with his conversation without waiting for me to nod in assent or smile, as though he hasn't heard my question,

—My little one, you're new to our group. Let me ask you, do you think there's a difference between those who under-stand life and others who feel it?

I wait for his riposte, since he clearly wasn't expecting a response from me.

—Doesn't the situation resemble someone who's trying to analyze a work of art? He concentrates on it for a long period of time attempting to pierce through it, understand it. Whereas someone else will sit back in a comfortable chair, admiring it from afar, relaxed, just to enjoy it. He isn't thinking about its size, its weight, its dimensions, the aesthetic errors, their occurrence, the reason it was created, and, and . . .

—Do you usually ask all these questions, or is it just the wine?

He laughs.

—Ah, the wine; don't condemn me from our first meet-ing—we have many more questions ahead of us.

Finally he pulls up a stool and says earnestly,

—I'm one of those who feel. I don't understand things, but I feel them. Sometimes, I don't want to understand things and I'm content to merely feel them. Do you know, if I concentrate by looking at a single strand of hair, an ordi-nary hair, if I hold it in my fingers and contemplate it for a while, I can imagine any split on its surface to the extent that I can draw it in 3D.

I distributed his words among the sculptures around me. I was attracted again to the wooden statue devoid of male and female features—or maybe it combined the two together.

He continued:

—What about you? Are you someone who feels or someone who understands?

I was certain now that it was the alcohol that had started to talk,

—I'm someone who follows her dream, guided by Madame. The problem is that I started late. I'm more of an amateur. I've never been a professional in any of the arts, and I didn't learn my father's profession until it was too late. I've become a mere sample of the diversity of fantasies.

—At least you have the choice to fantasize.

He placed the ashtray in his lap and lit another cigarette.

—Please continue. It seems that our group is expanding.

—Continue with what? The question is, will we be able to start again from the beginning, disregarding this destruction that has consumed seven years of the time we have to soar? Can you moisten the clay once again, and go back to the starting point?

He clapped enthusiastically:

—Ha, you've entered the maze of questions. I don't think I'm that drunk, I can see how white your teeth are from where I am.

I had a strange desire to allow him to see how white my teeth were from close up, but I stayed where I was, saying:

—I assure you they're genuine; not porcelain.

A satanic laugh emerged from the glint in his eyes.

—I love that streak of feminine wickedness.
He added:
—When it does no harm.
I asked him:
—Why sculpture in particular?
He was lost in another reverie, as though he, too, was rerunning this morning's military communiqué:

"In the early hours of this morning, the enemy launched a wide-scale attack against our forces in the region of Al-Khafajia. Our brave soldiers were able to contain this attack, destroying the invading forces in two stages. In the first stage, all the enemy's troops on the first four bridges were wiped out. In the second and final stage all the enemy's remaining forces on the fifth bridge were eventually destroyed."

The communiqué ended. He answered my question in a sarcastic tone.
—Because my aunt gave me a book for Christmas called *Mambo*. It was the story of a black African boy who worked with his father selling bananas. I was six years old. When I asked her why Mambo was black and I was white, she told me that our Maker made us out of dough using white flour and water. He then put us in various molds, like cake pans, and placed us in a huge oven to cook us. When the bodies were cooked, he took us out of the molds, glazed our skin to make it shine, and then sent us out into life. When the Lord was making Mambo and his kind, he mistakenly forgot them in the oven for a few minutes too long. Their skin got burnt a little and they came out like biscuits. My aunt died,

leaving me the tale of *Mambo,* until I decided that I, too, wanted to make humans out of water and flour. I ended up in the Department of Ceramics, specializing in sculpting.

He stopped briefly to blow out some smoke.

—And now, all that I remember as I head to the military barracks every morning is that one day I was a sculptor. When—I mean if—I ever get the chance to work again, I'll have lost the ability to sculpt. Definitely.

The word "definitely" resonated between us. He lit another cigarette.

—Do you know what I'm doing now while we're being shelled? I am making miniature models of the battlefields using sand, gypsum, and pieces of cardboard. The only difference is that I don't really know what I'm marking out. I don't have the right to ask where these sites are. I have to transpose these military maps that are given to me in the fastest possible time, without asking any questions.

The gold chain around his neck glinted in the candlelight. I moved closer to him and saw it was a small cross, hanging out through the collar of his shirt. He noticed what had attracted my attention. He lifted it up between his thumb and forefinger, smiling. "To keep away the vampires." We both laughed politely. As we were about to rejoin the others, he said to me softly:

—I'd love to see you again.

He then added:

—Without Madame this time.

Then he concluded by saying:

—We have to meet again.

We're continuously getting updates with the latest news from the battlefield: incursions by military forces across the border, new troop movements, maneuvers, the retaking of territories and shelling of sentry points with mortars and heavy artillery. The number of military communiqués has increased with bewildering speed. Civilians are convinced that we're heading toward the end. We're informed about the movement of ships in the area and the instructions handed down to the Port Authorities. There've been reported infringements and clashes, infiltrations and explosions. Protocols, ministerial letters, legitimate rights and agreements are being discussed, along with dated treaties and joint meetings. Military planes penetrate restricted airspace, and watercraft transgress the demarcation lines in Shatt al-Arab. An oil refinery has been hit and new minefields have been located. Another contingent of young men has entered the cycle of joining the training camps and military units, responding to the country's call in its hour of need. Cuts in electricity, water supplies, and telecommunications have become more frequent and more concentrated.

I learned to wait. I spread the day out as though it were a week, to fight slowness. When the phones would go down, I'd transfer my attention from my wristwatch to the calendar on the wall, which had my mother's appointment dates marked on it. She'd found a small lump, the size of a chickpea, in her left armpit. She described it as an "unpleasant feeling," and sometimes she called it an "uncomfortable situation." I went with her immediately to the specialist to whom our doctor had referred her. We entered the X-ray chambers and emerged from the labs that analyzed her blood and urine. A week passed by, then another. The results were incontrovertible: it was breast cancer. The specialist immediately recommended a mastectomy to remove the diseased breast. The other option was to go abroad and have the operation there. However, the formalities to get an exit visa took so long these days, he feared that the disease would spread further during the delay.

The announcer's face doesn't move, it's only his throat that's producing the news:

"The capitals of a number of countries have reported on the magnitude of the battles for the small town of Al-Khafajia. Strategic military studies presented by European military academies have confirmed that the battles our forces waged inside enemy territory were the largest-scale land battles seen since the days of the Suez War. These battles, and some of their lessons, are considered to be the most significant battles since the Second World War."

I spent the next few days shuttling between the hospital, the passport office, the directorate of residency and travel, the office for foreign residents, the British embassy, the bank, the lawyer's office, and the travel agent. I tried to come up with a speedy alternative for my mother. She spent an unbelievable amount of time gazing at her reflection in the bathroom mirror, or in her bedroom. I felt completely paralyzed, unable to respond to her calamity. I didn't know how to embark on a conversation with her or what to say. But she made the decision to submit herself to the anesthetist, saying calmly:

—Medical science in England won't change the fact that I have this illness. I have to face this situation myself.

She then added:

—There's no point making a drama out of my illness. Haven't we been through enough already?

I couldn't figure out if her coolness was a sign of resignation, or a self-enforced measure to cool down the fires in her breast, or if it was merely her English way to hide her emotions. It was what I'd come to expect from her in the past. In any case, I respected her courage in facing this new reality. She had to make a decision rapidly. This type of disease could not wait. She had to have the mastectomy now and she will have to travel to England later. She sighed and asked me to turn off the light and shut the door behind me. I stood in the corridor, realizing that I'd lost the ability to cry some time ago. She finally received the letters she was waiting for from David and Millie. They were now contracted to another oil company and were based in Saudi Arabia. They'd decided to settle down in the Gulf region. When they heard of her illness, they sent her a card wishing her a speedy recovery. On the front was a picture of a cute bunny in a doctor's white coat, holding out a bunch of blue flowers.

The television was talking about creating victory. It was discussing the decisions of the Security Council, the nonaligned movement, the principles of the nonaligned nations and the members of the Islamic Conference Organization. The reports reiterated the absolute necessity of continuing with economic and social development, and specific emphasis was placed on encouraging further economic progress with the resources available. Plans were laid out for a national strategy. The war had not only damaged numerous military establishments; several civilian targets had also been bombed, and nuclear reactors had been attacked. The announcements were followed by reports about the international black market that had emerged, trading in spare parts for F-14 fighter planes, Phantom, and F-5 aircraft, and Chieftain and M-60 tanks. We were shown maps displaying the sites of the latest battles, marking out Tehran, Mehran, Kasr Shireen, and the province of Arabistan. Finally we were shown images of explosions that had occurred locally. The victims had been students at the College of Administration at Mustansiriya University. The streets were filled with banners declaring their condemnation of the bombing, and we were shown images of the martyrs before they graduated.

I didn't realize that the success of my mother's operation was only the start of our struggle. Having a patient at home isn't like visiting a patient in the hospital. I felt that her emotional state was my responsibility. Entirely. I was afraid to reply when she said things about how her femininity had ended, about the new deficiency she felt and the emptiness that she carried around inside her. The sound of her gentle, interrupted weeping in the hot night, when the electricity was cut off, left me in a quandary. When I heard her whimpering in that distinctive way, I knew she was trying to clean her wound on her own. I entered her room once without knocking on her door. I was shocked to find her lying on her back, having exposed her wound to the air. Her right breast sagged away to one side; the left looked like something that a hungry cat had left behind. After that, she asked me to get a private nurse to look after her until she'd recovered fully. She then shut the door to her room.

. . .

The military spokesman's declarations continue:

"In the battle of Besayteen, the violent clashes have resumed. Several attempts were made to encircle our troops, but they all ended in failure. The enemy forces attempted to alleviate the pressure on their men at Besayteen by initiating new battles elsewhere along the front. They were unable to achieve their objectives because of the heavy losses they sustained. Our forces were able to once again raise our flag above the rooftops of Besayteen."

I received a handwritten note from Saleem, the sculptor, after a prolonged period when the phone lines were down. I read his words for the first time,

I'd like to see you if you don't mind.
I'm sorry, but all the lines in our area are down.

I had to wait another two days before I could see him, as we went through a period of intensified air raids. A curfew was imposed for forty-eight hours. He was due to go back to the front soon. He wanted to bid me farewell.

He took me in his arms before we'd reached the sitting room. Its mood was relaxed, with all those turquoise cushions. He insisted on calling me "my little one." He wrapped his strong arms around me and engulfed me in his warmth as he breathed in my scent. He devoured my face; it revealed a mixture of curiosity and surprise at the way he greeted me in the corridor. I could read the fear of the front lines in his eyes. He felt my quiver of anxiety at this rushed meeting in the face of an unknown future. He understood my amazement and drew me closer with a smile, as if to justify hugging me.

—We have no time for slow introductions.

He added:

—I'm pleased by your daring, your willingness to venture out when the city is under threat of further air raids; and I hear your mother has just undergone a major operation.

I smiled at what he was saying. At that moment, politeness fell away as we were both startled at the sound of shooting. It came from a security observation point nearby. As we settled down on the cushions scattered on the floor, I said:

—Yes, I left Madame to keep my mother company tonight.

He replied with no hesitation:

—I'm grateful to my friend, Madame.

He then added:

—I wish your mother continuous good health.

—I wish you the same. When do you return from the front?

He lit his cigarette, blowing out the smoke in agitation:

—That depends on the Fates. Anyway, I believe that I've looked upon a good omen when I looked into your face.

—What? Am I to become a good luck charm for the soldiers?

He did things without asking permission. He lifted his hand up and reached toward me, saying:

—Why not? Your presence here delights me, your questioning arouses me, and your age worries me. There's a lot of thinking material there for the long days in the dugouts, the nights on duty, and the hours of sentry service.

His hand settled between my hair and my neck. A

strange familiarity spread from the tips of his fingers and rolled down the curve of my shoulder. I tried to concentrate on the next question I had in mind for him:

—They say that a soldier's most difficult duty is keeping watch at night.

He replied:

—Believe me, it's the pitch darkness and the sense of responsibility that turns you into a different person until the dawn breaks.

—So what keeps you going?

—It's the knowledge when we are out there, that there's somebody waiting for us in the city; so we make all kinds of plans for when we come back.

—What about your family?

—My father has died. My mother lives with her younger sister in the North. I go to see them occasionally when the situation permits.

He added cynically:

—You see, I was conceived after fifteen years of infertility, and only after they convinced my mother to go and pray at the shrine of the Virgin Mary at Metti's Monastery. She was told that the prayers of infertile women were answered there. Now she has gone back to the monastery to pray for her only son to return unharmed.

I added:

—Safe and sound.

He laughed a little, as if to change the mood, and said:

—Would you like a cup of tea?

He was absent only briefly. The aroma of tea indicated that he'd prepared it before my arrival over a gentle flame. We sipped a small amount, surrounded by a halo of silence that was pierced occasionally by the sound of wild shots from the nearby security point. We were separated from each other by one henna cushion. I asked him:

—Do you think we'll have forgotten everything when this war is over?

—My little one, your questions are older than you.

—What about you? How much older than my questions are you?

He smiled with his heavy eyelids, then carried on:

—Do you mean, will we forget this war when it's over? Or that when this war is over, will we forget everything about ourselves?

From the flat's upstairs window, another military communiqué descended upon us, detailing the violent confrontations that had occurred to the east of Basra. Five major battles had taken place:

"Military sources confirmed that the size of the enemy forces that had gathered across the border in the Basra sector was unprecedented in the course of this war. The forces included eight brigades, among the best in the Iranian Army. They'd been withdrawn from their positions along the Caspian Sea. Their objective was to overrun the borders, take the city of Basra, and separate the southern areas from the rest of the country, but Basra, the second-largest city in Iraq, will not succumb."

He got up to close the window, reflecting on what we'd been saying, and continued:

—Yes, now that the war has reached this stage, it doesn't matter when it ends. Of course, the material losses will be added up. They will count the military, economic, geo-graphical, and human losses. The world will study this war, its calamities, and its effect on the region. People will look into the correct means of starting the process of reconstruction and returning life to the way it was before. But no one will ask about the results of this burning human desire to survive. If we survive, having lived through times when our youth might have been ended by a metal bullet no longer than one centimeter at any moment, we will undoubtedly forget what life was like before this war.

He then asked, as if he were talking to himself:

—How will we remember what we used to be like? How will we be able to retrieve from the past a time that has been consumed by flames?

A short while later he returns to my query again.

—We will certainly have forgotten everything about ourselves when it is over.

I asked:

—Then what?

His swollen hands enveloped mine, which had turned into a brown dove caught between two strange tense wings. With my free hand I caressed the upper part of those wings. The bulges were not swellings; they were the tendons of his wrists and hands, which had become prominent as a result of their repeated contractions and relaxations as he sculpted. He replied:

—A time will come when we'll have to create new identities for ourselves in order to bear the difficulties we'll encounter in civilian life, in a new era of survival.

—What would be the point of surviving like that? What would remain for us?

—Nothing other than the illusions that we'll find inside ourselves.

—What about you?

—This war has made me ask myself why I sculpt. I no longer ask myself why we live and why we die. Those kinds of questions only bothered me in the first few years of the war. Now that we've gotten over the initial shock, we've come to realize that it's a wheel of flame that we can't avoid. I'm now looking for my own personal illusion to escape. Will I survive with my sculpture?

It was as though I threw the question back in his face:

—Will you survive with your sculpture?

His hand is sweating over mine. The dove's feathers are falling away. Minutes pass. Time has no presence. He kisses my hand elegantly.

—I don't know why I sculpt. Is it to create lifelike images with my own hands? Even though they're still, they're my creation. I feel as though I possess them. Or maybe it's because only my eye can see my creation when it's a nondescript mass of clay. For example, I remove the layers and release the woman of my dreams from within it. Is it a game of creation, possession, or escape? Or a selfish game I play on my own? All these questions make the worrying times ahead even more complicated.

His last comment was somewhat confusing. I didn't elaborate. I remained silent. As I left his flat, he planted a gentle kiss on my forehead to erase the tension between my eyebrows. I left, bidding farewell to the unknown. Or welcoming it.

The news from Al-Muhammara is the first item in the evening bulletin:

"Last night, the battlefield became a flaming inferno, lighting up several kilometers of the surrounding areas . . ."

We went through difficult times in Baghdad as the shells flew overhead. No one was able to predict when the losses and the deterioration of the economic situation would end. I attempted to allay my mother's anxiety by trying to find her new bras that would fit her new appearance, and painkillers imported from abroad. How could I celebrate my first relationship, with a man ten years older than me, when we have no time for any questions? Is there time for a relationship in a time of shelling? How can we construct in the midst of destruction? One person after another is being mowed down. Buildings and homes are being brought down. Time has been brought down. Will he hold my hand again between his swollen palms?

The weeks pass slowly. I kill time by seeking out household necessities: foodstuffs and medicines, items that have become scarce or unobtainable in the present climate. When I find a few moments of relative quiet, I try to concentrate on translating a clipping from a foreign newspaper, or an article from a local paper or book, to maintain my linguistic abilities.

A tired voice announces:

"At ten o'clock yesterday evening, the enemy mounted a new incursion into our territories. Their forces crossed the international border in the region of Basra in a front ten kilometers long and penetrated to a depth of ten kilometers into our lands. At first light this morning, we were able to halt their advance and contain the momentum of their attack. Since ten o'clock this morning, our armed forces have embarked on a counterattack on the enemy's forces, inflicting heavy casualties on them."

Saleem's first period of leave was three days, from the time he left the barracks at Al-Mahaweel till he rejoined his unit. The phones were down once again. He sent me a brief note to arrange a meeting on the second day after his return to Baghdad.

He has left the door open for me. The electricity is out again, so he knows the doorbell will not work. I enter slowly, cautiously, frightened that my loud heartbeat will give me away. His beret and boots are by the entrance; his military belt is lying on the floor by the bed. A khaki shirt with a salty map under each armpit hangs beneath a larger map of calcified damp on the wall that he hasn't had time to deal with. Hanging from a thick nail, three black bats hide their human faces with wings like abayas. On one of the shelves is a spotted snake that is biting its own tail; beside it is a dried carnation that has no scent. A wide painting of lame camels is fixed on the wall. The only thing that separates them from the sands behind them are some lightly brushed cubic humps. I didn't wish to wake him from his nap amid a fragrance of chestnuts in the torrid heat. The window is open, admitting a lazy breeze. The curtains sway gently, alleviating the harshness of the dry heat. The mercury in the thermometer hanging in the corridor outside is creeping toward the 40°C mark. I stand in the frame of the door for a few moments looking down at him. He reaches out with his hand, his eyes still closed. He lies there, not opening his eyes, his open hand awaiting me. Soon I find myself underneath the mirrors.

My head is spinning. I'm with a man for the first time in my life. I'm frightened and cautious. No! It's said that caution and curiosity can't eat together from the same plate. I have to decide: will I be cautious or curious? The war is raging outside; we're here on the inside. We have no time for slow introductions. Why am I repeating his words? Where are mine? Did I lock the door to the flat behind me? We have just one hour; he wants to visit his mother this evening and is taking the four o'clock train to the North. His eyes invite me, like his swollen hands. The mirrors help us in getting to know each other. He asks me to lie beside him; he's smiling all the time, all the brief time we have together. His face comes closer to me; the mirror reflects his back. My arms have started to converge around his sides. I'm like a vine whose tendrils have started to grow around him. The mirrors reflect us together and breathe life into our bodies. He imprints the front lines on my lips.

In a flicker of a dream the color of the sky, I build myself a palace with walls of sugar. His smooth blond body is dripping beads of sweat that have melted the walls of my palace. I'm swimming in a milky white fluid. I can't escape; I surrender. Before I drown, I swallow a small wave of final sweetness.

The hour is over. I place my fingers down there and say to myself, Sunset Red. I don't cry the way they always did in the Egyptian films we watched on television every Friday afternoon. I am no longer his little one.

· · ·

Al-Fao. Battle of the Salt Triangle. Another batch of young men have been called up for military service, along with another group of Reserve officers. The ceremonies continue as badges of bravery are awarded to men who have excelled in battle. The televisions show us more prisoners of war sitting in the dust with their hands over their heads. Outside the health centers, queues of civilians gather to donate blood. The fiercest clashes since the start of the war continue. The human harvest commences at midnight. Clashes occur in the minefields; small, medium, and large maritime targets are struck. Field guns and mortars have been destroyed. The lenses of the cameramen show us close-ups of damaged microwave stations, satellite communication centers, a radar unit, and a missile silo. They're followed by images of a burnt-out rocket launcher, infantry positions, an ammunition dump, a lookout point, a fuel depot, tankers, and armored vehicles. The screens are now filled with sand dunes, but they fail to hide from the viewers the full horror of the final details. The camera meanders through no-man's-land to reveal the ugliest scenes of thousands of shredded human bodies. The voice of the announcer informs us that the Permanent Committee for the Victims of War at the Ministry of Defense has called upon the International Red Cross for its assistance in removing the rotting corpses from the battlefields where they fell. They fear the widespread epidemics that might engulf the region as a result of the rapid decomposition of these human remains in the heat of the southern sector.

I tossed aside the back issue of the *National Geographic* I'd been flicking through. The silver dolphins on the cover lay stretched out on the table. Suddenly that evening, my mother asked me:

—I don't mean to interfere, but are you still waiting for him to return from the front?

—Yes.

She grimaced—another pain in her chest.

—Are you contemplating marriage?

—What marriage? We've barely met!

—Even if the war ended?

—I don't know.

—You are Muslim and he is a Christian; that will create problems for you in this society.

—I realize that, I've thought about it.

—What about him?

—I think he'll drop the subject and see what the future brings.

She said in an almost mocking tone:

—The bravery required in civilian life may be greater than that required in the military. Anyway, avoiding marriage is the easiest solution.

—Nothing is easy, Mother.

She added:

—You're wasting your time.

—You mean I'm wasting more wasted time.

She gazed at me for a few moments, then said:

—Maybe you're right to answer me that way; after all, you're the war generation.

—Regardless of this war, my feelings for him are strong.

—I can see in your eyes a longing to settle down—that's why you have to be certain of his feelings towards you. The ball usually starts rolling in the man's court.

She added after a brief while:

—In spite of the fact that he's an artist.

I asked her:

—Why this serious tone, Mother?

She adjusted her seat and took a sip of water.

—Maybe it's because I want you to avoid unnecessary pain.

I reflected for a while, then asked her:

—Mother, is this discussion about me? Or about you?

She smiled with a strange serenity.

—No, it's merely an inquiry to find out if you're truly in love, or whether you're going through an emotional crisis, which has been transformed by the war into a form of love.

I waited for a while, hoping that the question springing to my lips would dissipate, but went on:

—Was that the way your relationship was with David? Was it your distress that transformed emotion into a form of love?

Our conversation was interrupted by a military communiqué from the radio in the kitchen:

"Our warplanes and military helicopters accompanied our ground forces during their battles today. The total number of sorties on this day was a hundred twenty-seven by our warplanes, and twenty-eight raids were undertaken by our military helicopters. All our warplanes and helicopters returned safely to their bases."

She returned to my question after the communiqué. I didn't expect her response to be so calm. After drifting away in her thoughts for a minute or two, she replied, as though her voice had returned from a distant place:

—Now that I've lost half of my femininity, I can probably discuss this matter. Why not? Your father has died, God rest his soul; and David claims that he was forced to leave the country. Therefore, in my dreams, I see only absent lovers.

I didn't know if I'd been right to bring up this topic. She held her hand over her empty breast as she continued:

—Millie keeps sending me those silly cards to cheer me up as though she's apologizing on his behalf. She can't comprehend that I'm in a different world now. All I really wanted was to find him there by my side when I came around from the anesthetic.

I asked her:

—Did he promise you anything?

—Promises, my daughter, are a mere figment of our imagination. Just as your father promised when he was a student in England that life with him in the East might be "alright." We were discussing our youthful prospects and the possibilities for our future at that time. How those days resemble old photographs I thought I'd discarded in the closet of my memories.

—And David?

—This time David thought that returning to the West might be "alright" after we'd lived through this experience in the East together.

—So, what happened?

—I think the difference between us was that his thoughts were those of a bachelor.

—But you were still prepared to follow him in spite of your attachment to us.

—Do you know, I can no longer tell if those feelings I had were a desire to follow someone, or a need to get away from someone.

She added:

—Maybe I should say, I don't know if I was contemplating fleeing to a new situation or fleeing from a situation.

—Is this the way you would describe a marriage? A situation that can be changed when we're fed up with it?

—Don't condemn me. I'm merely relaying my experiences to you. Let us not be judgmental. Suffice it for me to say that your father, in spite of the distance that separated my western upbringing from his eastern essence, if he were still alive, wouldn't have left my bedside till I was myself once again.

She then added, as though she was severing the link between us:

—All I wanted to say to you was, there are some truths that are only discovered when it's too late.

I realized that she was leaving our discussion in my court. I gave her a tranquilizer and said to her:

—It's quite possible that you'll be granted permission to travel to England. She readjusted the way she was sitting a second time, and drank down her glass of water in one go. With a slight tremor in her voice she asked:

—Will you be coming with me?

I did not hesitate, nor did I think of the consequences of my decision. I simply said:

—Yes.

Communiqué:

"In response to the enemy's savage bombardment of our cities, our brave forces have replied with daring air raids on the enemy's economic targets. However, we lost two of our planes in these raids, and we hereby hold the enemy responsible for the well-being of the two pilots."

He didn't return the day he was entitled to his leave. Abu Sa'ad, a messenger from his unit, knocked on our door. He gave me a letter and the keys to Saleem's flat. Then he left, having declined my mother's offer of a cup of tea, saying he had to return to his unit. My heart started pounding, fearing the worst. I opened the letter. It was more like a telegram:

My little one,

I've been transferred to Mansouriat Al-Jebel. My leave has been canceled, but I've been promised an extended period of leave next time. I haven't been transferred to the front lines. I'm still blessed with the task I've been set: to produce military tables that I don't question. There are, however, rumors from my friends who draft the edicts that I will be assigned the task of returning the bodies of dead soldiers to their families. The key to the flat is probably in your hand at this moment. Scent the place for me with your breath until we meet again. I hope that I'll find you waiting for me this time. I send you a kiss, à la Rodin. Don't worry. Abu Sa'ad will keep us in touch.

The voice of the newscaster follows me like a nightmare:

"In the battles that the enemy embarked upon, a number of enemy soldiers were taken prisoner. It has emerged that among those prisoners are a number of children whose age does not exceed sixteen years. The Red Cross has been entrusted to return these children to their families, and has been asked to draw up a report regarding the enemy's actions in sending these children into the battlefield."

That night, I once again met Hassoon, the little fool from my childhood days. He started dancing in front of me with his little penis sprouting from underneath his dishdasha, pointing it in all directions, proud of the fact that he'd placed the spout of the broken bottle around it. There was no sign of any of the other children or the beer factory. I called to him to ask him where Khaddouja was. He ignored me and started running toward the fields. I chased him, begging him to stop running, but he kept going. He was halfway there when he tripped on a rock that had suddenly sprung up underneath his feet. He fell hard onto his face, striking the ground. I caught up with him, out of breath. I kneeled down beside him. I was calling out his name, but he was not answering me. I turned him over onto his back. He'd lost consciousness. His little penis was swimming in the dust, in a pool of blood near his belly.

Two weeks later Abu Sa'ad returned. Saleem's leave had been canceled once again until further notice, according to the rushed messenger, who assured me that all was well. I read the letter curiously.

My little one,
What can I say! He rested on my shoulders all the way to Basra. I made my car bear what couldn't be

borne; my soul didn't know its depths till that
moment. I discovered the limits of my endurance
on that final journey. A trip that the soldiers at the
front call "a duty." I'm crawling up the road that
has started to lose its shape. My fingertips feel like
cotton wool and the flesh covering my bones feels
so soft; it's as if they have melted in some places.
My feet feel disconnected from my ankles. They've
been separated from the rest of my body as they
swim about in the darkness underneath the seat. I
prod the pedals at random; the speedometer
responds by vibrating on its axis.

The officer is a kind man. He wished me patience
and a safe journey. Above my head is the box I lifted
up with my breath. My car moves forward like an
elderly tortoise weighed down by its heavy shell,
the way I'm weighed down by the coffin above me.
I'm in the same state as the car; I'm walking on all
fours. I can no longer bear to think. Every time I
recall his dismembered body being transported in
that oblong wooden box, the hairs on my scalp
stand on end and I feel them piercing my skin like
needles.

The ringing of the phone interrupts his words. Its reso-
nance reaches me from the depths of a deep well. I abandon
the letter. It is Madame, in a jolly mood:

—We'll call the show *Light*. The National Theater will
provide the dancers from their troupe; I'll provide them
with the music and the choreography.

—Congratulations.

Another communiqué. I try to concentrate on the rest of the letter. The result of the operations was the destruction of the enemy forces. The topic under discussion now is economic growth alongside the rifle. An article calls for social progress, the correct upbringing of the nation's youth, and encouraging construction, brick by brick. Another article emphasizes that the war is being fought not only on the front lines but in civilian institutions: the schools, hospitals, and government offices.

I'm sure that the vehicle has slowed down intentionally, and that the edges of the pavement are coming together to impede our progress. Attempting to switch the radio to another station is pointless. All I get are verses from the Koran, a military communiqué, greetings from the soldiers at the front to their families, a patriotic song, or the hissing of a station that has gone off the air. I vomited a small amount of froth through the car window. The yellow stains intersect the orange stripe on the side of the white car. I distract myself by counting the quivering mirages that follow each other on the asphalt of the road that lies ahead of me. Ghosts of the heat—I rip through them, and they rip me apart till we reach the first military checkpoint. The sergeant asks me for my driver's license, my permit to travel, and my military service book. An explosion in the road had affected the flow of traffic. When will these calamities cease? I delivered the martyr, or what remained of him, to his family. Nights without end have gone by and I've been unable to sleep; so I write to you. Forgive me if you find that I've become a different person.

• • •

His second period of leave was slightly longer than the first. When he laid his head on the pillow, I could tell that he'd changed. He was saying so many things; it was as if he was delirious. He asked me to stay with him as long as possible. We remained together the entire ten days. The only time I left him was when I checked on my mother. A nurse remained by her side, and Madame visited her at my request. I felt as though all I had was those ten days.

It was a period of dancing, two lips swaying above and two below. Something was ending, and something was about to begin. We laid our heads on each other's chests until our breathing became synchronous. We counted the minutes under the droplets of cool water in the tub. The smell of peaches emanated from the creamy soap. A plastic green frog from his childhood floated on the froth in the bath. I stretched out. He sat facing me. He held a drawing pad and a carbon pencil in his hands. He was muttering to himself; I could hear snatches of what he was saying: "How did the gods dare to send you to me at a time like this?" He was going to sketch me, or parts of me. He stopped for a moment. The time between us seemed an eternity. He threw down his pen and notebook, they slid from his hands into the washbasin. He sat down on the floor beside me, one hand in my hair, the other creating dolphins in the water around me. With my eyes closed, I threw my arms backward. I liberated a dove the size of a clenched fist; it clapped its wings and flew off from beneath my armpit.

Images from the battlefield. A soldier has been captured. He's placed in front of the cameras. His clothes are dusty, his features indistinct. His arms and legs are bound with ropes to a military vehicle on the right, and another on the left. Both vehicles set off in opposite directions. They're swallowed by the edges of the television screen. We face the remains of what was once a human being.

That night I heard a repetitive banging. I thought he was sculpting in the studio. I didn't wish to disturb him in his isolation, while he was working. I tried to synchronize my breathing with the banging, hoping that the rhythm would take me off to sleep once again, but after battling with insomnia I made my way to the studio. Half his statues had been shattered by the blows of his hammer in the early hours that night. He was sitting in the far corner gazing at the wreckage, smoking greedily and crying.

I made my way toward him carefully, trying to avoid an injury to my bare feet from the scattered debris. When my shadow reached him, Saleem looked up at me. He grabbed the hem of my nightdress, taking strength from the cloth. He pulled on it to lift himself off the ground and said with a strange calm:

—In the past, I could recognize in myself a feeling they called the birth of creativity. Now all I feel is a brief revival in this struggle against time, like the fleeting last moments of consciousness before an inevitable death.

—I want to hold you before it's too late.

He stretched me out on his empty workbench. We occupied it till dawn. Painfully.

He bade me farewell and left. I tidied the flat and shut its door behind me. I decided to walk home after the long enforced curfew of the past few weeks. I took Al-Kindy Road, walking past the central post office, which had been destroyed by the last missile. It was a small building, adjacent to the local Rafidain bank serving the residential area. All that remained were crumbling bricks, protruding metal bars, broken glass, and a black banner bearing the names of the two employees who had lost their lives in the attack. They say that the firemen retrieved the two bodies in four stages. I walked past an electricity pylon bent over at its center. I stepped over a brown stain of dried blood. It had congealed like a map over the pebbles under my feet. I picked up one of the splattered stones; it left a gap in the map of blood. I stood there for a few moments contemplating the ruins, then with all my strength I hurled the little stone toward the leveled building. It traveled through the air, attaining the farthest point it could reach, and eventually settled amid the debris around it.

Before the end of Saleem's next period of leave, we decided to take up Madame's invitation. We went together to see her performance in *Light*. She was at the peak of her brilliance and anxiety. She'd spent the last two months training the forty youngsters of both sexes from the National Theater troupe. This would be her finest hour. She'd given up on having her own dance troupe. They'd become history—a forgotten dream after the red curtains went up for tonight's performance. She must have compromised on her standards for artistic perfection and accepted the constraints of the current circumstances. I found that she'd made use of the slim bodies of her students instead of bemoaning the fact that they lacked the fitness for a ballet performance. His swollen hands held mine in the darkness of the hall.

The performance started with two groups of dancers separated by a river. The first group prospered, blessed by a gentle golden sun, unaware that the other group was coming down with a disease, as their sun was hidden away by a thick cloud in the shape of a giant mushroom that occupied half the area at the back of the stage. The dark cloud persisted and couldn't be dislodged. Those living in its shadow decided to leave, seeking the warmth of the sun elsewhere. They arrived in the land of the shining sun, but a violent war soon broke out between the two groups, both claiming possession of the benevolent sun. The music raged, the casualties started falling into the river, the battle continued for several days, till the music reached its climax. As it hit the highest note, a water nymph emerged from beneath the stage. She tried to offer some of the purity from her world to the warring factions. It was Madame, who leapt up wearing a shiny white costume, resplendent as a legend. She swam between the points of darkness and light, her steps following the rhythm of the music, or maybe it was the music that followed her steps.

She had applied all the theories she'd taught us about lighting and shadows. She flew through the air, imploring the dancers through her graceful movements to join her in contemplating the falling light. She danced for the two adversaries amid the falling rays, revealing to them that the light was a gift for everyone and didn't belong to one group or the other. It was a blessing that they should not be fighting over. With the grace of an expert ballerina, she explained to them that light entered the eye and did not leave it. Were it not for this fact, we would be unable to see each other. If the warfare continued, the sun would be angered and the curse of darkness would ensue. The music became melancholic, the dancers were scattered on the ground as they followed her around cautiously. She then asked them to imagine the opposite. What if the light emerged from their eyes and fell onto objects to illuminate them for us? What if the gift of vision were an individual attribute that each individual possessed separately? Using the music, she started to point to the stronger members of the group, and then to the youngest ones, and finally she pointed to the student who was playing the role of the invalid. One person's vision was stronger than another's because he was younger or had a stronger body or was in better health. Could you imagine a life in darkness in which we lit up our days and our nights with rays emitted by our eyes?

Suddenly all the members of the group stood up and forty pairs of eyes shone in the darkness. It was a stunning theatrical effect achieved by using fluorescent tape around each student's eyes. The water nymph asked them to imagine what this frightening tunnel vision would be like. Our vision would take the form of dark tunnels lined with black, and we would see light only at the end of these tunnels when the light from our eyes fell onto the objects around us. We would look at the chair in the corner, or a car passing by rapidly, or part of a building or a garden, or a field, or the face of a friend or a loved one. Madame swayed amid the rays. On the backdrop, images of inanimate objects danced about in the emptiness behind the dancers. The image of a chair floated past. A moment later a modern sketch of a speeding car descended, then part of a building appeared, and a strip of a green field flitted past. She danced for them, asking the question "If the sun departed, we would die in the tunnel, and our lives would lack a beautiful horizon, so what would we do then?"

A sadness settled on the audience. I understood then that this was to be her final performance. I admired her beauty from afar. I wasn't sure whether she was dancing for her dream or for her mother, who hadn't left their house since the day of her divorce. Her father was of Iranian extraction. When they separated, he'd taken his son with him and headed to Tehran; her mother had kept her here. Maybe she was dancing for her only brother, who was fighting in the Iranian Army. She hadn't met him for several years; Shatt al-Arab had become a barrier between them.

When the applause and the cheering died down, we met. She told me that she was going to marry a retired violinist who was fifteen years older than her. She added laughingly, "It doesn't matter if they allow me to perform tomorrow; my mission has ended. In any case, a late marriage is better than an early divorce."

She turned toward us:

—You two are the first to be invited.

Saleem squeezed my hand, saying:

—Do you know that a year has passed since we first met?

I was surprised.

—I hadn't realized you were counting the days.

He said:

—It's a sign of the times. What's the next step for us? Even Madame has decided.

I laid my head on his shoulder.

—I'm leaving soon with my mother for England.

Amid the commotion and the shootings, the Goodwill Commission and the Committee for Humanitarian Endeavors both realized that the war could continue for several months more. They put forward the following proposals:

1. The full withdrawal of the armed forces from the territories.

2. The formation of an Islamic Committee, funded by the two countries, that would look into a solution to the conflict.

3. The formation of a committee that would determine which party instigated the war as a prelude to deciding who would be paying reparations to the other.

My mother asked me as we were eating breakfast together:

—So, am I going to hear wedding bells, or what?

—Mother, please, you know that in our tradition we don't ring bells at weddings.

She answered me in that mocking tone she has adopted recently.

—In your tradition or his?

She then added in her usual calm manner:

—I wonder what he'll fear more—his family, or the prospect of commitment?

I lost my temper.

—Why are you trying to make a joke out of this?

She replied without any hesitation:

—On the contrary, I'm trying to tell you that you don't have to accompany me to England if you think that your life here with him will be better.

I didn't have an answer to her questions. I'd had no time to myself. Situations had been forced upon me and decisions had been made on my behalf. It was as if my mother and Saleem had laid the plans for my future between them, and I had no power to object.

After a period of quiet and reflection, she said, as if she were talking to herself:

—In any case, it's only the most intelligent who can avoid making a mistake before it's too late. But on the other hand, only a fool would let the most beautiful thing in her life slip by and miss the chance.

The war ended, Madame got married, some of the prisoners of war returned, some of the soldiers lost in battle emerged, some of those present disappeared. Flights from Baghdad International Airport were resumed. I left the festivities celebrating the cease-fire behind me. I cast a final glance at the statue Saleem had carved for me and the note he'd sent me with it to avoid saying goodbye. Saleem took the train from the front to the North directly to rejoin his mother. A soldier I didn't know delivered the statue to me in Baghdad. Abu Sa'ad was not our go-between this time.

My little one,

As you see, it's the outline of a man who has driven a stake into the ground. The shadow of the stake is laid out on the vast base beneath him. He measured it with his hands and realized that it matched the length of the shadow, but whenever he tried to measure its length against the length of the shadow by laying it down directly on the ground, the shadow vanished beneath the recumbent stake, and melted into its pores.

My little one, I'm sorry, I feel that I'm too old for you. Do I have the right to withhold you from the life that lies ahead of you? I know that you'll understand my position, maybe in ten years' time. Glide away, my little one, this is your time. As for me, I will stay. I will stay in this place where I've learned the various skills I need to kill time, and I didn't realize that the final blow would come from time itself. My God, how did we not realize that time + time = eternity!

Cross to the other side. Travel far away. Roam the lands. Seek . . . maybe you'll find a just settlement with the soul.

I climbed the stairs to the airplane carrying my one suitcase. I'm followed by my mother with her one breast.

6

Autumn in Hammersmith. The main road overflows with
cars, crawling silently down its left side. They stop at the
traffic lights, at the entrance to a convent called Nazareth
House. As the lights turn amber, the queue oozes out
slowly from the side exit, heading toward West London.
Skeletons of moving vehicles pass beneath my window on
the first floor.

I look vertically downward. I watch the passersby; their
plastic hats and waxed overcoats shine. They dart between
the dried leafless trees, which resemble medieval broom-
sticks that have been planted upside down. The desiccated
trees stretch out in a regular pattern all along the pavement. Their branches are like hands, whose fingers have
stiffened as they point skywards. The raindrops run down
between the dried twigs and bounce off the domes of fluorescent multicolored umbrellas. The florist takes her plants
back inside the shop. I see a sign offering driving lessons
to nuns and priests—WELCOME AFTER SUNDAY PRAY-
ERS. Other posters: AIDS, ITS CAUSES AND DANGERS.
HOW WOULD YOU PROMOTE A WAX MUSEUM? DO YOU
FEEL LONELY? WOULD YOU LIKE A PARTNER CHOSEN
FOR YOU BY A COMPUTER? HOW TO GET RID OF AN

UNWANTED PREGNANCY WITH NO PAIN. USED PIANOS FOR SALE.

I accompany my mother to Charing Cross Hospital, where she'll have further medical exams. She'll be treated by Professor Karl, who specializes in breast cancer. His office is on the sixth floor of this building, which has been designed in the shape of a crucifix. On our way to the hospital we meander through the small concrete tunnels intended for pedestrians crossing under the bridge as they head out toward Putney. The walls of the underpass have been paved on the inside in blue ceramic. Someone has sprayed in big bold black letters TRAMPS HAVE THE RIGHT TO TRAMP, DAMN YOU! She smiles. We try to avoid each other's eyes. She is fearful of what awaits her.

In the West Wing, we sit in the waiting room with the other women patients. A young nurse enters swiftly; her movements are soundless, apart from the licking, rubbing motion of her shoes on the modern plastic tiles of the waiting-room floor. She walks past us silently, after having nodded to acknowledge our presence in a respectful manner. She removes a tray of leftover food from one of the side rooms, replacing it with a breakfast tray. I couldn't see its contents, as she held everything above my line of vision. One woman wears a colored turban; another woman palpates with trembling fingers the bare patches on her scalp where the hair has fallen out. An elderly woman enters, leaning heavily on two crutches as she progresses slowly toward an empty seat beside a bald girl. The needle in the girl's left arm is connected to a bag of fluid, which hangs from a mobile drip stand. My mother sighs, "My God, it's a hotel with a funereal flavor," as she follows the nurse who has called out her name. Her blood and urine will be tested, and X-rays taken to assess her state of health.

I enroll in a course to improve my spoken and written English. My mother will be spending most of her days in the hospital, or in its attached departments. My English language school is in a small building across the road from the South Kensington underground station, the area where London's French community resides. Near the classes of the Department of Translation is a small café. It's here that the crowd of young foreigners gather. They represent every country, creed, color, accent, every cultural, social, financial, and religious background. The place is called the Reptiles' Corner. It's so crowded that when London's miserly sun appears, once every week or two, it seems to me that every couple has only one shadow between them, following them as they go by. There's no sign of anyone English here.

The sound of a kiss makes me turn around. Youngsters walk past kissing on the street—two fish clinging to each other by their mouths. The Africans walk swinging to a secret rhythm. The French delicately consume a cheese made from frogs' milk, with style. A student whose father is Indonesian and mother is Norwegian wears a necklace made of little yellowed skulls, each the size of a fingernail. He flirts with a German girl wearing a dress as beautiful as a peacock's tail, who has a voice as ugly as its screech. The owner of the café is a very talkative soul. He offers us biscuits made with black sesame flour, saying, "Ah, if I were in Italy now, I'd go snail hunting with my friends, especially after these heavy rains we've had." Blond, ginger, and dark profiles sway gently in each other's shadows. Their owners admire the chalk paintings of the pavement artists. The artists wait for pennies to be thrown into the battered hats they've left alongside their paintings. A Portuguese youth hands out necklaces made of dried pepper seeds to his friends. He claims that his hobby is figuring out who's wearing contact lenses, while one of his friends is telling everyone about a newly invented laser-driven mousetrap!

I occupy a seat in the left corner of the café; a large lady has just vacated it, and it's warm. Her folds of fat dance as she walks away, leaving an aroma of sandalwood behind. A Japanese girl is writing a letter. When she finishes, she dips a delicate finger into the cup of tea on her table, passes it around the inside rim of the envelope, and seals the letter. I pick up my Arabic newspaper to read the news from the East; a slice of lemon floats in my cup. One of the students comments in faltering English, "Hey, you read from right to left, don't you?" I reply with a smile, "Yes, except our newspapers—we read those from left to right." But he didn't want to know more. This morning, I didn't hear the news on TV before I left. I was thinking about my seat on the upper level of the double-decker bus; would there be a seat at the front? Closer to the sunshine? And I'd forgotten to buy my paper before getting on the bus. Now I read the headlines: "New Border Disputes in the Gulf Region"; "The United Nations Condemns Iraq's Invasion of Kuwait"; "The Assets of the Conflicting Nations Have Been Frozen!" I gulp down my tea; it drops straight to my stomach. I lift my head, looking around for a familiar face to save me, only to see a few youngsters in the café wearing headphones, listening to their Walkmans, communicating with hand gestures. I leave the place immediately. At the bus stop a green sign catches my eye: PLEASE PUT YOUR RUBBISH OUT HALF AN HOUR BEFORE THE COLLECTION TIME—THE REFUSE COLLECTION AGENCY. I'm annoyed by a child who entertains himself by blowing bubbles through a straw, into a fruit juice packet, instead of drinking it.

The next day, the United Nations declares that all commercial links with Iraq are suspended. Naval forces are to be sent to the Gulf region. That is followed by the declaration of an economic embargo. The mobilization of armies and military aircraft has started. I enter my mother's room to find her lost in her daydreams. A ribbon of light from the window at my back quivers on the wall in front of me. The fan moves the curtain with its breeze so that the band of light is disrupted, at certain moments the fabric of the curtain is reflected onto the wall.

—It's September in London—how can you turn on a fan in this weather?

She answers in a voice that seems to come from another world:

—It's the thought of the chemotherapy that the doctors are recommending. It makes me feel so hot I am almost choking.

She then adds, as though she's just remembered:

—Have you heard the news of home?

—Yes.

After a little while I ask her:

—What are we going to do?

She answers:

—Exactly what we did last time. Nothing.

—But Mother, this is the twentieth century; the weapons of modern warfare have reached their peak in causing death!

She looks at me for a few moments. Then the contact between us is broken. She turns her back to me, indicating that it's time for her to rest. She says, in a low tone, as though she is under the influence of a strong sedative:

—Let us pray to God then, that modern medicine has also reached its peak in saving lives.

She slept.

I spend a time full of emptiness, between the hospital and the Reptiles' Corner. I flick through the newspapers and magazines in both languages. Fear of the military buildup, threats, and orders to withdraw are the topic of conversation at all gatherings. From early August until January the next year, time seems to stand still, a hostage to the final deadline laid down by the president of the United States. During that period all telephone communications and postal services with Iraq cease; travel is forbidden at the country's borders. I breathe in the days with anticipation; in one hand I hold all the analyses of the current situation; in my other hand, the latest results of my mother's medical tests.

I head toward the Portuguese market with one of the students from the language school. I want to get away for a while from the questions I face from everyone in the café about what I think is going to happen. We go past some shops—smells of leather and fish emanate from them. I can almost distinguish how salty the different kinds of fish are. An acidic aroma pervades the air of the indoor stalls around Camden Town. Hills of fresh walnuts cover mounds of dried fruits. Discs of dried bananas, apricots, a paste made of dried raisins, varieties of yoghurts with strawberry flavors, and raw sugar cane. The ceiling is decorated with fishing nets. A rudder of a ravaged boat. The remains of an old warship. A ship's spoked wooden wheel with brass handles hangs on one of the walls. Stains of black smoke smudging its edges. Hands exchange chains of pearls, corals, and trinkets made of amber and mother of pearl. Bracelets made of tortoiseshell. I close my eyes, inhaling the fragrances, wishing it was the Shorja market in Baghdad.

A television screen flickers in the corner of the shop. A map of the Middle East is laid out, decorated with groups of tanks, armored personnel carriers, military units, equipment, and soldiers. Caricatures of the American president and the Arab Nations compete to make it onto the covers of the news magazines. Live coverage of the daily activities from the area flow from all the media channels. The soldiers in the American camps send greetings to their families at Christmastime. A brief shot shows them brushing their teeth in the desert near the Saudi borders; they rinse their mouths out with bottled mineral water. One of the customers coughs in my ear. The correspondent reiterates the statements of the delegates gathered in Geneva. Behind him the camera films the famous water fountain in the lake as it flings its spray upward. The voice of peaceful reconciliation is very soft, but the countdown to hostilities is loud and clear.

The military forces sent to the area now number 400,000 men from the Allied nations, who are preparing for the initial assault. The meetings of the ministers and their discussions regarding "the Nineteenth Governorate" have overrun the international newspapers and radio stations. I place a slice of bread in the toaster, watching the images of the western hostages and their children being released. The square piece of toast springs out, scattering crumbs over the headline in the newspaper—"Final Deadline Approaches." Beneath it in smaller print is another headline: "Proposals for Negotiation, and Failure of Negotiations." And on the last page: "Congress Grants the American President the Right to Declare War."

I attend the last gathering calling for peace on the cold night of the fifteenth of January. Youths have gathered and are shouting in Trafalgar Square. They're calling for a cessation of hostilities, an end to the killing of innocent people, an end to the starvation of children, and a halting of the armed intervention. Guitars are playing sad melodies; voices are singing in the name of Jesus. Everybody holds up candles to banish the darkness; the banners are everywhere; the temperature is below zero. We warm our hands around the weak flames from the candles. The sky is as clear and pure as the prayers, which are floating toward the heavens in every language and religion. The deadline is at midnight in America; dawn, 5 A.M., in England; and 8 A.M., early morning, in Iraq. The Americans tie yellow ribbons around oak trees, hoping for their sons' safe return home. The Iraqis tie green ribbons around the Shrine of the Imam al-Hussain, praying for God's protection. In the coldest month, the coldest war of the modern age is declared.

This is the city of precise appointments, credit cards, and stock market reports. Explicit magazines on display in the newsstands in Soho; shops which sell nothing but socks; American hamburger outlets selling Coca-Cola and various types of instant teas. A spate of interviews with young people defending their relationships with people of a different race. A black man and a white woman, a black woman and a white man. One enters a red public telephone booth to make a phone call with a ten-pence coin and emerges loaded with a bewildering array of business cards: "Fifi Provides You with a Personal Service"; "Leggy Blonde"; "Marble Arch Beauty Invites You to a Far Eastern Dream"; "Have You Experienced Japanese Charms?"; "Unhurried Thai Service"; "Your Warm Lady Calls"; "Your Pain Is My Pleasure"; all with accompanying phone numbers and photographs of bronzed and metallic bodies graphically displayed. It's still the city of traditional drinking establishments with unusual names: The Pig and Whistle, The Snail and Lettuce, The Fox and Hounds, The King's Head. It's the city of taxes, unemployment, and homelessness, where the drinking water is extracted from the sewers. The taverns swallow the working classes. They spread out the exhaustion of the entire week, seated on the pavement every Saturday and Sunday. Men and women exchange glasses of beer over the wooden tables and illicit narcotic powders underneath them.

———

THE MAN IN FRONT OF ME has a facial palsy affecting the angle of his mouth. His seat is facing mine on the train heading toward Fulham. He eats a sandwich, and it seems as though he can't feel the saliva that is dribbling down from his droopy lower lip. After a while he takes a soft piece of bread from his sandwich and wipes his saliva with it. He then eats the piece of soft wet bread and burps quietly. When I reach the hospital, my mother is signing some documents which appear to be important. I peer at her from behind the curtains that surround her cubicle on the female section of the ward.

In spite of the success of the mastectomy she had in Baghdad at the appropriate time, the doctors were talking about their fears that the remaining malignant cells could spread to the areas surrounding the breast. They had decided to offer her a course of chemotherapy, an attempt to stop it from proliferating, or at least to spread her chance to live over a longer period of time.

She smiled and said:

—I have signed the consent forms for a course of chemotherapy. It means that I'll have to come to the hospital every two weeks for tests and intravenous fluids and other pleasant surprises. I'm afraid I'm going to be a bit of a burden to you for a little while. I know it's an especially bad time for you now, when you're so worried about the news from your country.

Her anxious tone doubled my worries:

—Are you in any danger?

She altered the way she was sitting:

—Not yet. Unexpected emergencies may declare themselves as the treatment progresses. For the moment, it's just a question of having my temperature and blood pressure taken. My blood sugar, cholesterol levels, and the chemical elements in my blood have to be monitored; I need to be given intravenous fluids, tablets, and other medication. Anyway, I might be lucky, since they may let me keep my other breast.

I took her hand in both my hands and kissed it. She pulled it away quickly.

—You can do that when I become unconscious. I'm not used to having you kissing my hand.

—My kiss came with my prayers that you will regain your strength and that your hand will not need any assistance from anyone.

Her voice softened a little:

—Thank you, darling. Don't worry; the nursing care here is first-class. I will be surrounded by women of my generation with similar conditions. As you see, almost all the instruments and monitors seem to have wheels on them. Even the telephone can be pushed across the ward! We have magazines, television, and music. I won't be lonely on this floor always full of people coming and going.

I left her, the fluid dripping slowly into her arm, each liquid meal lasting twenty-four hours.

The first air raid on Baghdad is being broadcast live on BBC television. John Simpson is describing the sound of the bombing and the black smoke that has started enveloping the city. The American pilots return unharmed to their bases in Saudi Arabia. Iraq does not retaliate; it merely resists the American air strikes, which are meant to wipe out the Iraqi Air Force before the start of the ground war. Twenty-eight Allied nations. Military aircraft of the most modern design with protruding snouts and wings as thin as notebook pages. The Post Office and the Ministry of Defense were among the early targets. The young pilots announce their complete satisfaction. One of them comments, "Bombing Iraq was like lighting up a Christmas tree!" Another pilot says, "The first attack was like a game of football. At first a player hesitates because he's afraid and hasn't got any self-confidence, but after you press the button for the first time, you get into the game and start attacking." A third pilot describes his share of the bombardment, saying, "I transformed the area into flaming balls of hellfire!"

Birds of steel pierce the skies in double and triple formations. They travel at low altitudes to avoid radar. Others travel above the clouds, incommunicado; the local people call them "crows of death." A few peace demonstrators wrap themselves in white shrouds and lie on their backs outside the White House. "Stop pushing the Buttons of War" they chant. The communication satellites transmit full coverage of what's being called "carpet bombing." The military whales are sent in. The undersurface of their bellies opens up in the air; the explosive devices tumble out, adding to the destruction on the ground. They help in unrolling the fatal carpet. Discussions continue, confirming military superiority, accurate technology, and the remote-control aspect of modern warfare. Water supplies and electricity are cut off as a result of the bombing of the pumping stations and generation plants.

Images of Baghdad. In the morning it's choking in the thick smoke; at night it's illuminated by balls of fire that roll around on the television screens. The news reports are crowded with information about trenches, levers, vehicles, ammunition, tools, tanks, transporters, towing equipment, diggers, wires, explosives, camps, and experimental training. Forty thousand tons of explosives have been used so far. News reports from Washington indicate that Americans everywhere are glued to their television screens. The restaurants have no customers. Everyone is preoccupied by the war; the number of crimes committed in the past few days has dropped dramatically.

On my way back to the flat I read in an English magazine: "Hell is a box whose lid has been opened." Images of civilians and soldiers wearing gas masks. Strange creatures with menacing looks emerge from the eyes sheltering behind the two small windows in the rubber mask. Protective padding for the nose, and similar padding for the mouth. A long plastic trunk hangs down from the mask, terminating in a valve. The protective garment is merely a fabric of chemicals, narrowed at the waist, and tethered at its ends to form wide trousers for the legs and thick gloves for the hands. Also in a magazine is an article describing the effects of mustard gas. It leads to a swelling of the eyes; the afflicted person feels as though his eyes have been covered in mud. It was developed by the Germans in the First World War. Another article describes the horrors of nerve gas, which attacks the nervous system, leading to spasms, convulsions, and eventually death. Scientists claim that it kills within fifteen minutes. If the afflicted person isn't aware that he's been exposed to the gas, or even if he is, the mask is useless once it's happened. His body will fall to the ground.

7

I scatter segments of my disjointed time among the Reptiles; sometimes I sit in my usual corner, at other times I
join them in their wild dancing—a flailing of limbs in all
languages. One of them once said to me jokingly, in a polite
French accent, as he knelt in front of my table, looking up
at me:

—Oh, pretty Mademoiselle, I beg, forget your sadness. I
would die for you.

—Then I will buy you a ticket to the Gulf.

His friends explode into insane laughter. I laughed with
them for a long time that night—until I cried. At the end of
the evening he put his arm around me.

—I'm new to this area; my name is Arnaud, I arrived in
London this week. I've rented a humble flat two floors
above this café. Are you from here?

—I am not from here, nor am I from there. That is the
problem.

He laughs in a distinctive way,

—I doubt that you have a French father and an African
mother like me!

—That explains the combination of your dark skin with
your aquiline nose. Anyway, you can say that I too, am the
product of a contrasting mixture.

He shrugs his shoulders:

—Then let us drink a toast. To confusion!

He lifts his glass.

—I might join you some other time. I have an early commitment tomorrow morning. Good night.

I distract myself with a small piece of malleable red wax. A short while ago it was the wrapper around a ball of Dutch cheese. I knead it into a small cube, then a heart, then a flower. When the phone rings, I throw the wax onto a plate and head to the hospital. Professor Karl spoke to me about the side effects of the treatment. He asked me if I could commit myself to looking after my mother when she returns to the flat. "Most definitely" is my reply.

He proceeds, while viewing my mother's chest X-ray:

—Your mother has agreed to undergo an experimental treatment with a chemical substance called Taxol. It's extracted from the bark of the yew trees that grow on the Atlantic Coast. Its availability is limited. We have a sufficient amount, which will be given to your mother on an experimental basis. If this treatment yields positive results in a number of patients who have agreed to participate in this trial, it will then be marketed commercially in the hope that it might stop cancers from spreading.

—Is there anything that I can do?

—We want you to encourage her to eat, because she will lose her appetite dramatically and dangerously. Her body will need protein to withstand the treatment. You will also have to look out for the side effects: fainting episodes due to a sudden drop in blood pressure, unexpected bleeding, allergies, rashes, and red spots on the skin. We will give you a detailed list.

. . .

I receive the first letter from Madame.

My friend,
   Someone has promised to send this letter to you via
Jordan. You must have a clearer view of the situation
from where you are; we live endless days with
cuts in the supply of electricity, running water,
communications, and other services. The important
thing is that we are still alive. An unending chaos of
fear, terror, and darkness from the black mist we open
our windows to in the morning, until the darkness of
the night, which commences every evening with the
sounds of bombardment that have now become so
familiar.
   People are fleeing with their families to and from
Baghdad. We do not know when the final knockout
blow will come. This event which you are calling
"Invasion Day"; we are calling "The Day of the
Glorious Summons." You have called this "a border
dispute"; we have called it "Reuniting the Province and
the Motherland."
   The Suspension Bridge, the heartbeat of the city, lies
disemboweled, each half drowning in the Tigris. We
awaken to the sound of the air-raid sirens, and we spend
the evenings using lanterns to dispel the darkness. The
economic embargo has placed the price of bread beyond
the reach of most people. Prices are escalating; petrol
has become a scarce commodity.

I rearrange the flowers that I've bought for my mother from
the florist on the ground floor, saying:

—The doctor tells me that you've signed the consent forms to undergo chemotherapy with the experimental drug Taxol.

—Didn't he also tell you that the disease is otherwise inevitably fatal?

—Don't you want to defer this for a while, Mother?

—This isn't the first time I have been used as a guinea pig.

She sighs, then adds:

—My God, how am I going to fight this disease?

—The same way you fought so many other things in your life.

—I can no longer remember what I fought against in the past.

—Have you forgotten your loneliness, the strange culture and language, and the unbearable heat?

She rests her head back on the pillow, as though it was too heavy to hold up.

—I've never in my life felt that I am such a failure as I do now.

She continues, talking to herself:

—I failed in so many different ways. I became pregnant with you by mistake, and I failed to correct that mistake . . . please don't misunderstand me.

She says that as though she was becoming delirious.

—Then I got married . . . and I failed to make my husband happy . . . Then I emigrated, and failed to understand my husband's culture . . . Then I loved a man from my own background behind my husband's back, and even there I failed, and could not keep my lover.

Her summing up of her life resembles a telegram, its seg-

ments separated by sighs composed of the word "Then."
Finally, she adds:

—My God, then what?

—I speak to her, trying to calm her down.

—Mother, we need a little bit of patience, as Father used
to say, isn't that so?

She carries on, as though she hasn't heard me,

—How can I believe that what is happening to me is a
punishment for what I have done, when I never believed
that there was a God guiding me?

I say to her:

—But he is here, Mother; he listens to us.

—It's too late, my daughter. I bade the Lord farewell in a
small church on the outskirts of London just before I joined
your father; my belly grew with every passing day.

She gazes at the ceiling for a while, then adds,

—I stopped belonging here when I left England and decided to try and belong to the East. In spite of all my efforts,
I could not belong there either, and now that I'm back here
again, I find that I no longer belong to my original homeland. Everything is so different.

—Why are you talking like this, as if tomorrow will not
come? We have so much time to correct the past, and to
talk about these things.

She smiles helplessly.

—It is a foolish notion, this question of belonging. We
only belong to the shadows of our bodies which follow us
around as long as we're alive.

My mother's cycle continues for months under the supervi-
sion of Janet, the nurse specialist in toxicology. A large mass

of confused femininity with two protruding green eyes and exceptionally well-looked-after fingernails. Her limbs are stout. If one of her hands was replaced with an average-size woman's foot, no one would notice the difference. Her voice is so deep, it has the huskiness of a young man's voice—a young man who's reached puberty only a week ago. She doesn't move or behave like the rest of the nurses. She circulates through the ward without an assistant. Her two bulging eyes make her look like a frog that has crept out of the pond, leaving its other inhabitants behind. When my mother introduced me to her, I secretly nicknamed her "Zakiya"—a seller of dried mint. Janet looks for a vein in my mother's arm. She inserts the needle; the fluid starts to drip very, very slowly. She then gives her an injection to fight the nausea, and a few hours later she comes back to give my mother another injection. This one counteracts the shortness of breath that accompanies the treatment.

I watch my mother as she dozes and reawakens with a detached attitude. I move from the visitors' room to the television room to the cafeteria on the first floor, and then back to my mother's bedside. Sometimes she complains of pains in the roof of her mouth; at other times she has a sudden attack of diarrhea and I have to accompany her to the bathroom. Her heart rate drops, or her blood pressure; I run to the nurses' station. Quite often she complains of numbness in her fingers, or her toes. She whimpers from the pain in her joints and muscles. When she realizes how much she is complaining, she says:

—Forgive me, my daughter, I feel so tired. My body has become so sensitive, even my fingernails feel so heavy.

Then she falls asleep again.

. . .

After a lengthy silence, I receive another letter from Madame.

My friend,

I came across a picture in a magazine of two huge planes mating in the air by means of a petrol refueling hose. Fuel planes follow the fighter planes in a strange symbiosis across the sky. Modern technology fornicates over our heads, is that not what this is? Whereas for us, using a car is now reserved for emergencies only; people are bartering with petrol instead of money.

It's raining bombs. You can't imagine what we're going through. A black rain covers the gardens, the streets, and the rooftops, resembling black decomposing remains; it makes the days uglier than the nights. The economic embargo has made us cut our hair short to economize in the use of soap and water. The communications tower above the Central Post Office was brought down by the attacking planes. Car bombs devour; a young man looks for his fingers blown off amid the debris. A dog carries its discarded paw as it hops three-legged across a ditch—the water a dirty pink color.

So many people are dying of heart attacks brought on by this ever-present fear. Women pray to God, "Do not dishonor us in our death . . . Do not dishonor us in death." Young women no longer sleep in their nightclothes. They dress up to go to bed, or wear their work clothes. They fear the major air raid, and are worried that they won't have time to put on any clothes

to preserve their modesty. We jump at the slightest
noise in the house. People are calling us "the startled
generation." I can't say that I wish you were here at this
time; but I miss you.

I try to phone her that evening. Eventually, I'm fed up
with listening to the eternal drone of the operator: "Please
wait, your call will be answered shortly, thank you." At
three in the morning, I wake up with a start from a brief
dream. I'd been roaming through the back streets of London, stealing contact lenses from the eyes of anyone who'd
fallen asleep. I lifted their eyelids with a pair of tweezers,
stole their lenses, and ran. In another scene I was at the
gates of the Karkh Islamic Cemetery in Baghdad, begging
the gravedigger, his rusty spade resting on his shoulder
on his way back from the grave, for my father's lenses.
He refused to give them to me. We heard a loud explosion
from the direction of Abu Ghraib, and a giant black cloud
shaped like a mushroom rose above our heads and advanced
toward the sky.

My mother is crying. Her voice awakens me, dispersing
the black smoke. I leave my dream in my bed and enter her
nightmare through her open bedroom door. As I run toward
her, I see she is holding strands of hair in her hand. She
holds them up to me, saying:

—Look, look what is happening to me. My beautiful
hair, it's all falling out!!

She puts her hand up to her head. Hair comes away without any resistance. Another lock is loose in her fingers. She
breaks down sobbing, her shoulders heaving with emotion.

—My God, what have I done, to be treated like a cat?

I try to comfort her while hiding my amazement.

—Don't be embarrassed—they warned us that this would happen.

Her eyes are wide with fear. She looks up at me, her hands still clutching strands of her hair.

—Talk is easy. I can't imagine myself bald, with one breast.

All I could think of to say to her was:

—It's God's will; what can we do?

She starts to sob again loudly:

—If I'd been born with your eastern emotions, I would have killed myself rather than suffer this humiliation.

After I cleaned her room and Hoovered away the fallen strands of hair, I tried to calm her down with a glass of cold water. She lay down quietly in her bed. Her eyes staring blankly into emptiness. I say to her,

—Do you think this cancer is hereditary?

She replies without looking at me:

—Maybe . . . Luckily for you, though, through my experience, you have the chance of discovering the relativity of life and death before it's too late.

She then adds:

—In any case, I hope you have inherited from me nothing but healthy cells. I ask you not to become engulfed in the trap of pessimism.

The next morning we receive a letter of complaint from our downstairs neighbor for having used the vacuum cleaner at an inappropriate hour.

About a month later, my mother starts complaining of headaches. Her sense of taste has altered. She winces whenever she's given an injection. Her body has become very weak and she spends hours sleeping. The voice in the elevator announces that we have reached the sixth floor. It has become a part of my daily routine, going up and coming down. I know all the notices on the walls by heart. The permanent ones no longer attract my attention. I now notice only the temporary ones.

As I enter the female ward, I smile at the six patients placed neatly on both sides of the room. In the first bed by the door is Angela, a spinster in her sixties. She moans silently, hardly moving at all. She is wasted to the bone. Her hair is always pulled back in a green hair band. She has no visitors, but every now and then someone sends her flowers. Her thin lips have a bluish tinge. She is always smiling sadly at the others. They call her their dear guardian.

In the second bed is a large lady. One can't believe that her breast is diseased. Her stout body gives the impression of a healthy pink glow. Underneath her nightdress, battling for room with her big belly are two engorged breasts, like balloons about to burst. Her name is Helen; she's always chatting about her husband, a retired pilot whom she's left on his own at home. She worries about him constantly, an elderly man in his seventies with breathing difficulties. His life is dependent on the oxygen cylinder attached to his respirator, which is fitted beneath his wheelchair. She is more concerned about what her husband has had to eat that day than she is about her cancer. If he doesn't ring her, she is annoyed and starts filing her yellowed nails while humming a Sinatra song.

The programs about the green gardens of Scotland, and harpsichord music from the eighteenth century, are driving me to distraction. I flick through the channels searching for news. The pipelines are spewing out their oil into the waters of the Gulf, causing the largest oil spill ever and threatening the ecosystems in the region. Experts are pondering how to clean up the oil spill, depending on the water temperature and the weather. If the movement of the water in the Gulf increases, shaking the oil, lumping it together, it will become less dangerous and begin to disperse. Fears are raised about the possibility of fires, which might erupt as the length of the oil spill reaches twenty miles. Rescue teams are sent to help the birds caught up in the oil slick. Emergency centers are set up in the area to wash the black oil out of the birds' feathers and the congealed grease out of their red eyes. The subject causes great sympathy and distress around the world. Everyone is talking about the poor birds whose wings have been weighed down by the heavy oil in the midst of this war zone. The images of these bedraggled animals are transmitted repeatedly by the world's media for several days. In the end, the experts agree, they can only clean up the area with a military operation. They have to use explosives to blow up the pumping stations that connect the oil wells to the coast.

Diane comes in; she is a Belgian volunteer worker. Her job is to befriend the patients, raising their morale. She tells them her life story, which varies from one bed to the other. She's an expert in treatments using scented oils and massages. Her personality changes selectively as she bonds with the various individual patients. Sometimes she accepts a tip from underneath the white sheets for her conviction. She has an amazing ability to distract a patient from her sorry state for half an hour or longer. She tells them about her Scottish grandmother, how she fell in love with an Irishman, following him all the way to Shanghai where he was working, at the end of the nineteenth century. Or about her husband, who used to hypnotize her to dispel the depression she would get in the winter from the long, dark nights and the miserable weather in London. He could make her feel the warmth of the sunshine when she awoke from her trance. Another story was about her twin sister, whom she looked for for twenty years, and then found on television through *Surprise, Surprise*. She is proud of her relationship with a wealthy elderly lady who died about a year ago, leaving her half her fortune. The other half went to her turtles, which she had spent her life raising and training. Diane had taken them in, giving them a new home in her garden. When the red hands on the clock divide its face into two equal halves, the gifted storyteller bundles her oils and fragrant ointments and her entertaining experiences into her little bag. As she is about to leave, she pins a badge on her chest which reads FRIENDS OF LIVER DISEASE PATIENTS and heads toward the Eighth Floor.

The last locks of my mother's hair have fallen—the leaves of another autumn. The world on the sixth floor increases my feelings of isolation. Creatures from a distant planet. Women who understand the daily routine of life beyond that big window overlooking the Thames, but cannot comprehend what is being taken away from them here on the inside, that which sits inside the chest. I observe nurses through the window, running down the outside corridor, its far end blending into the skyline. I speak to Anne, the new patient admitted to the ward as an emergency. She was given Bed 4. Her cancer has spread and reached the liver. We are unaware that she will be leaving us in a mere two weeks. Introductions in this world are based on the nature of the disease and where it is growing. That is what differentiates one woman from another. Anne was a nun, in her fifties. She counts the beads in her rosary with her right hand while her left receives the colorless intravenous fluid. Her fair complexion has slowly started to acquire a yellowish tinge, which eventually spreads to the whites of her eyes. She tells me to come and sit beside her to kill a little time. She asks me:

—What do you do with your life?

—I translate documents, and I look after my mother.

—Your mother is lucky to have you around. Are you married?

—Not yet.

—Do you fear solitude?

—I fear that she will no longer be with me someday.

—But do you believe in God?

—When I need him, I feel that he is near.

She repeats after me, like an echo:

—He is near.

Then she adds:

—Ever since my twentieth birthday, when I decided to become a nun, I pray every night to the Lord, and thank him for the peace he has bestowed upon me that I may help others, guide them and advise them. I knew a time when I was at peace with myself, a calm that endured for thirty years.

She hangs her rosary on the drip stand and continues:

—But now this frightening jaundice has put a mountain between me and my soul, tunneled by a little river, no wider than my finger. I cannot see the other side, but on my side of the mountain there is a steep ascent. I see its foundation, but not the heights, and my little river can't contain me; my days and thoughts float away on it.

She sighs a little:

—I feel as if I have failed the Lord after all these years of devotion and lessons in accepting Fate. It is a war, my little one, a war.

Before I leave Anne, I say to her:

—I too will pray for you.

—God bless you.

She makes the sign of the cross in the air above my head. I leave the room. I feel a tightness in my chest. I get myself a can from the drinks machine. The heat is stifling in these hospitals. The ventilation is minimal and the windows are firmly sealed.

The local news is that thirty-five Iraqi students have been arrested in England and will be held as prisoners of war until further notice. The news report confirms that each student will be provided with a prayer mat and that they will be served food prepared by Islamic methods. They will be treated well, far away from the press cameras. The Jumhuria Bridge has been brought down by the bombardment, and the Nasara Church in the Bab al-Sherji area has been hit. Direct confrontations have commenced; the victims have started to fall. A long line of prisoners of war are herded toward the Allied troops, eyes blindfolded, hands tied behind their backs. Their clothes are removed and placed in plastic bags.

One of them bites into a bar of chocolate. The helicopter pilots continue their "search and destroy" missions. They describe the abandoned tanks that were destroyed by the bombing as "sitting ducks."

Anne died; she was followed soon after by Angela, who wore her green hair band till the last. A sad silence settles over the remaining women. The ward has become a collection of patients' beds; the only separation between a woman whose life has ended and the other women whose lives are approaching their end is a thin curtain with dull blue flowers. Even Diane's attempts to console the remaining women are of no avail.

My mother's condition has deteriorated with the passing days. Her illness is covering every single item in the list of possible side effects, in sequence. Pinhead spots appear, spreading over the entire affected area. The doctor diagnoses this as early signs of skin cancer. He left her bedside assuring her that Taxol was the best medication available in the country at the present moment. She thanks him quietly and continues to flick through the pages of her magazine—*Hairstyles for Women*.

Mr. Jeffrey comes onto the ward; they all call him Jeff, or Jo-Jo. He is a young man in his thirties, thin and petite, who leaves behind him a whiff of sweet perfume. He skips daintily through the corridors, bending over and kissing the hands of his favorite female clients. He is the hospital wig maker. He visits the department once a month, takes the women's orders, and makes them an excellent imitation of their original hairstyles, until the crisis caused by the chemotherapy is over, and their own hair starts to grow

A SKY SO CLOSE

back. Jeffrey would cry when he found out that one of his dear friends had passed away. He would then dry his little nose, the result of high-quality plastic surgery, on a little handkerchief with the letter *J* embroidered on it. He was prepared to spend a whole hour with one patient. He would wait for her to choose the hair that suited her complexion and age from the magazines displaying his artistic accomplishments. He would become very animated as he suggested the appropriate color, length, and style. He carries with him a golden mirror with a distinctive handle shaped like a fish's tail. Rumors abound that he is eagerly awaiting his father's permission to have his relationship with his partner blessed. His boyfriend, Ralph, works in the laboratory for sexually transmitted diseases. Helen insists that Jeff is the sweet face of the tragedy of the future. She refuses to allow him to measure her skull with his soft hands.

The television channels are still showing segments about the war's dimensions—its causes, and the psychological state of the returning Allied soldiers. They talk about the services that are extended to them out in the desert. They are offered free phone cards to contact their families at Christmastime. Familiar music is broadcast to them from Saudi Arabia, on specially set up radio stations, to allay their sense of isolation while they're far from home. On that special day, they are offered fruit cake and a choice of meals at the Army canteens. On a second channel, a series of outbursts are directed at a number of European politicians accused of arming the region. Other revelations involve drug dealing and sex scandals in South America. Images show the return of embassy employees and some

212

students to Iraq, and there's a program on Indian cooking. After midnight, I watch reruns of old newsreels from the day the Rasheed Hotel was struck, when the receptionist was killed at her desk by falling debris. This was followed by detailed reports of the bombing of the industrial area in Zafraniya near my childhood home; the western Allies suspected that the area was a site where chemicals were being produced for military purposes.

My mother calls out to me:

—I forgot to give you this letter. It arrived for you this morning.

My friend,

It's not easy for me to describe to you the way things are deteriorating here day after day. We're living in a state of complete mental disarray. We've lost the ability to direct our lives, as our choices rapidly diminish. Our lives are dependent on the lifting of the economic blockade, which would allow us to catch our breath; but on the contrary, the situation worsens. What is being said in your part of the world?

My own personal circumstances I will describe as a cipher. I read a lot to escape the emptiness of my private life. My mind wanders away from one word to the next. My eyes drift from the page to the colored vase on the table in front of me; the print floats away into a blurred colored cloud and I can no longer distinguish between the page in the book and the edge of the vase.

Sometimes I get a crazy feeling that there is a little lizard by the side of the cushion I'm sitting on.

Whenever I look at the text, I imagine that he has stuck his head out and is watching me. So I have to keep glancing to the side of my cushion to confirm that the lizard is only a figment of my imagination. On another occasion, I was halfway through writing a letter to you when one of my eyelashes fell onto the page. It clung to the tip of the pen, and the page became stained with ink. For no real reason, I lost my temper and started cursing my misery. I ripped the letter to shreds, and I still don't know why. An explosion went off nearby, and I found myself under the sofa.

By the way, carbonated drinks have become items from another planet, they are so expensive. Farouk, who sends you his best regards, said to me, "Madame, it's been months since we burped!" The poor thing, how he longs for a bottle of Pepsi-Cola! Some car hire firms have been converted and now hire out women. Cultural activities are heading for extinction. Hunger and culture compete with each other, and we've come to know boredom very well. Private ventures and businesses are dying, one after the other. Unemployment is increasing with the rising prices and the fall in the value of the dinar. People in the streets are confused and everyone asks what the future holds. Depression is available for everyone, free of charge. How far I have come from the first lecture I attended in Russia when the speaker told us, "Our artistic life span is brief, therefore we must develop our bodies rapidly." I can hardly believe that I am midway to seventy. That is how cynical we are when describing our ages these days.

· · ·

I wish that row of palm trees would disappear from my dreams! I had spent a very long day with my mother; she had revealed to me the extent of her malignant illness. The breast that had recently become affected was swollen and disfigured. The site of the breast that had been cut away had become ulcerated and was secreting a purplish fluid, with yellowish encrustations. She showed me her misery but asked me not to gaze for too long nor to come too close, as the smell of her festering sores was pungent and repulsive. She added:

—It is brave of you to look upon me in this state, but daughter dearest, try and remember me when I was at my best.

Her fingers are swollen. Her fingernails have started to change in color and her joint pains have increased. Her cheeks become rosy for two days after each course of treatment and she is prone to the most trivial of illnesses as she has lost her immunity. She asks me after long thought:

—How will you manage your affairs on your own?

—God forbid, Mother—what is this pessimism?

—Leave your emotions aside and answer me. Are you planning on returning to Iraq?

—I don't think I would do that in the present situation. Madame's letters have given me an idea of what going back would be like.

—How will you live?

—I've been promised a job at the translation bureau at the start of the new year. The new post has been allocated to me.

—Thank God for that. At least your childhood confusion between the two languages was not wasted. I wish your father were still alive to witness your ability to stand on your own two feet.

—I never thought I would end up becoming a translator in London.

—And I never thought I would spend my last days a cripple.

—Who says you're a cripple?

—The pains in my back say so, my dear.

We have lunch together. I try to encourage her to eat more proteins. She prefers soup with soft bread. She asks me to open a tin of cold pineapple for her. She chews on a piece slowly and calmly. I can't tell if this is a moment of contentment, or total resignation. After that we watch *Casablanca*. We drink tea, and she dips her favorite Scottish shortbread biscuits into her cup. She says:

—If people died in groups . . . hmm . . .

She remains quiet for a brief moment, then carries on:

—If we all died together, do you think we would still be afraid to live alone?

I wasn't expecting that kind of question in the middle of the film, which I thought she was watching intently.

—What is all this talk of death from one minute to the next?

She ignores my objections and carries on:

—Isn't that the truth? That death is such an individual thing. Therefore, people prefer to live with others to avoid being killed by solitude. Why should human beings live in solitude, when they are going to die in solitude? Yes, why should one live alone, when they are going to die alone? Doesn't this same instinct push us into relationships, marriages, and having children? Is it not to store in our subconscious images of our children staying with us, finally walking behind our coffins at our funerals?

At this stage I ask her:

—But what if we all died together as you suggested, Mother?

She readjusts the way she is sitting. She hits the cushions, repositioning them behind her back:

—In that case, I think that it would be easier for someone to choose to live on their own if they wanted to, or to bear the loneliness if they found themselves with no choice.

—What do you mean?

—It seems to me that loneliness would be easier to bear if we knew at least that we would die in a group.

—How?

—It's like the feeling you get when you're about to cross the road. We subconsciously wait to cross with other people, not on our own.

—Sometimes, Mother, I just don't understand you.

She answers in a tone that mixes reality with resignation:

—Now . . . is our last chance to understand life . . . because very soon we will cease to be.

8

Bloated Helen died. Her final hours were like the death throes of a cow. I used to say a prayer for her every night before I left the ward, until I found her bed empty that weekend. My mother was sad at the loss of her chatty friend. They called in her husband, the disabled pilot, to say his farewells to her. A nurse wheeled in an old man in his seventies. He looked stunned as he sat in his old-fashioned wheelchair beside his wife's bed. She was completely unconscious. He'd brought her some red flowers. He held her hand and spoke to her softly and gently, spreading out his farewells over two whole hours, until it was time for his oxygen cylinder to be replaced. He was overcome by his emotions and started to cry as he was being wheeled away. He reached out, hugging the catheter bag that hung from the end of her bed, maybe because the bag was the closest thing to his wheelchair, or because it contained the last warmth of her body.

I looked for Arnaud, the Frenchman from the Reptiles' Corner. He was coming down the stairs from his flat. I met him as I crossed the threshhold of the café. I needed a strong hot coffee. He flung his arms open wide:

—Oh Mademoiselle, where did you disappear to?

He planted three kisses on my cheeks. He put his hand in his pocket as he smiled, saying:

—Oh, before I repeat the mistake I made last time, here is my phone number. It's so easy for you to disappear.

I was refreshed by the energetic tone of his voice. After the coffee we agreed to spend the weekend together. We arranged to meet for a meal in a small French restaurant, in one of the corners of Leicester Square.

A bland dinner tray arrives at my mother's bed. She has become an anxious creature who walks with the aid of a wooden stick. It has been her constant companion recently. She uses it to point at objects to her right and left. With its hook, she picks up one of her garments, which has been thrown over an adjacent chair, then drags over a box of tissue paper from the far end of the mobile hospital table. She has even started to use it to attract my attention. She then hangs it on her chair's wooden armrest. Spiky hairs have started to sprout through the sagging skin of her scalp. They give her the appearance of a pale hedgehog. She spends half an hour in total silence as she combs a wig she has fixed onto a doll's head made of white foam.

A lady doctor with a slender nose and extremities is with my mother. Her fingers resemble long French beans. She moves them around as she talks quietly to her. I have arrived at the appropriate moment.

—Have I missed anything?

My mother says:

—This is my daughter.

The doctor:

—In that case, bring your chair closer.

She carries on:

—As we explained to you from the very beginning, the cancer cells can move from one breast to the other. This is exactly what has happened. Now the danger is that it might spread to the base of the spine. This is what we suspected when we saw the black spots on your bone scan and when you developed this weakness in your legs. We never promised you, of course, that this disease would leave your body, but our hope is that we can delay its spread. We will concentrate on alleviating the lower back pain, and we'll also increase the tablets to help with the nausea.

My mother is not listening. I try very hard to concentrate on the doctor's lips and the present moment, avoiding my own thoughts. My mother has gulped down some air, asking for water to wet her throat. She holds on to the white plastic container intended for sudden bouts of vomiting. She says to me unemotionally:

—It's a pity. I thought I would live another year to enjoy what time I had left, even if it is very brief. But now it seems I won't be going for a walk in Hyde Park again.

I stayed with her till Saturday night; then I went for a walk with Arnaud in China Town. We swept our gaze across the graffiti crawling along the walls as we walked past on our way to the restaurant. A madman standing on a marble staircase waves to us. He thinks he is on an escalator taking him upward. On the street corner, an elderly man sits outside the entrance to the underground station. He is using his fingers to push the teeth of his upper jaw, making sure they haven't come loose from his gums. Beside him a young girl is crouching down, peeling away thin layers of her fingernails. Arnaud threw them a few pennies; their jangling in his pocket had annoyed him. We headed toward the nightclub where those seeking pleasure spent their nights until dawn.

We enter the dark cavern; its tables are wooden barrels covered with green-and-white-checkered tablecloths. A green candle on each barrel, along with an earthenware plate of olive oil, garlic, and ragged pieces of French bread. A strange hideaway underground with an atmosphere of eternal sunset.

After several hours of eating, drinking, and dancing to the tunes of the accordion, a corpulent man stands up. His stomach is overflowing with wine and his pockets are empty at the end of the evening. I'm feeling slightly dizzy as I watch him from where I'm seated. His obese body moves heavily between the bar stools. He reaches out, feeling his way forward like a blind man, seeking out the last few drops of wine left behind in the glasses of a group of young men who've recently departed. A human being without a circumference, he has no height and no width. His body's folds relax lazily, one above the other, as if they are steps leading down from above, from a neck without dimensions. I say to Arnaud:

—Which one of us do you think is more drunk, that man or me?

When Arnaud looks around, the fat man has picked up an ashtray. There are a few drops of alcohol in it, as someone had poured wine over a cigarette to put it out before leaving. The fat man put his finger into it several times and is now sucking the ashes soaked in wine. Arnaud pays the bill. He pulls me by the hand, saying:

—Come on, I don't like these sights.

We walk in the street, exchanging kisses and laughter. We go past another man lying flat on his back at the corner. His head falls, thudding against a rubbish bin. A greasy liquid and unpleasant smells are seeping out of the bin. I know then that I'm definitely in London. I say to Arnaud, "Let's steal his lenses and run away!" The man's purple hair stands up, like on an electrocuted cat. Arnaud shakes his head and laughs,

—It's obvious you're not used to French wine!

He lifts up his index finger and points in the direction of Piccadilly, saying:

—That's the bus we have to catch.

I feel even dizzier. I can't see any bus . . . Is he talking about that red telephone box sliding forward slowly on its back?

I ask him as we climb the stairs:

—Have you ever been so overcome by a need for a person that you can't bear to leave them?

He replies heatedly:

—Not since I turned thirty!

I feel my body swaying with bittersweetness. I lean my head on his chest.

—Are you going to show me how the Reptiles make love in their Corner? Or will you sleep on the couch like a gentleman?

—I know that you're physically and emotionally exhausted. We can postpone it.

—Ah, you are mistaken my friend—this is your best chance to seize me.

He smiles at me and says:

—Who told you that I wanted to seize you? I want you to walk into the room on your own two feet.

—In that case, there's no need for you to carry me.

He doesn't answer me. I shout, as if this warm feeling that I'd known him for such a long time gave me the right:

—I'm sick of playing with myself, listening to my own voice, alone.

He bites into half a cake stuffed with apricots that has been left on a pink plate on the table as he heads toward the kitchen.

—Did I tell you that I hate pastries?

He shouts back from the kitchen:

—Coffee with sugar or without?

—Bitter please . . . because, as a child, I once forgot some dough in a closed box for several days. When I opened it, I found it covered in green fur. I can never forget its awful smell!

—Refusing pastries wouldn't go down well in France.

—By the way, I forgot to buy a toothbrush this morning.

He smiles as he reenters the room:

—You insist on playing to the absurd.

—Your coffee won't stop me.

He sits beside me on the sofa.

—Is it true that the French have the most unusual romantic escapades?

He throws back his head and laughs for a long while:

—I don't know if that applies only to the French. But the most unusual experience in my life was making love to a woman who was a complete stranger. I knew nothing about her and she knew nothing about me. We were together for a whole hour in a darkened room without even the light of a candle. When she started shaking as she lay beneath me, I felt a wild, savage happiness. But her shaking continued with weird sounds. I found out a short while later that she was an epileptic and had just had a minor fit.

We laughed and let the coffee go cold.

We spent an hour together. What happened wasn't unusual—no fits and no weird sounds. We welcomed each other like two old lovers, each married to someone else, who meet once a year by candlelight.

My friend,

Our children, these little beings that we have created, are no longer able to sleep soundly. Their thoughts have become filled with violent images of real war in all its blackness and redness. Nightmares shake their beds with the sound of bombs and air raids, they see visions of raging fires from underneath their bedroom doors. Daily life has become like a series of photographs passing quickly through our memories, stopping at the end of the day with the image of a deserted, burnt-out tank. A metal sculpture that had been chewed up by steel teeth and spat out onto a beach of broken glass. We can hardly believe that this is really happening to us!

The West describes this as "Desert Storm"—we call it "The Mother of all Battles." Round tables that spin around themselves. We've lost all the features of modern civilization, except our bicycles, which have become the cheapest form of transport. We try to avoid the streets overflowing with the stench of dying frogs. *Alef Ba* magazine has a caricature showing a civilian

trying to get back to his home. The drains have
overflown, filling the street, and he is saying, "I pity
Vincent, from the TV series *Beauty and the Beast*. How
did he bear the smell of the sewers?"

We've acquired new habits. Shrapnel stopped us from
sleeping on the rooftops. We are put off eating fish;
polluted from nibbling corpses in the Shatt al-Arab
River. Some people have started sleeping with their
mouths open. They fear sudden death from the
transmitted blast injury of a nearby explosion. You see,
a story went around that two lifelong friends became
separated when a missile landed on the Qadasiya
district nearby. One of them died because he was
listening to what his friend was saying; the one who
was talking survived because his open mouth allowed
the blast wave to travel through his body without
causing internal injuries.

Isn't it strange the Americans are calling themselves
"Desert Rats"? We always thought of them as the
"Nivea Cream Soldiers." Did you hear the story of the
young man who placed a note to his sweetheart in his
mouth? He was in the Amiriyah shelter, which was
struck by a missile; he realized he was going to be burnt
to death with his friends and family as the walls started
collapsing over their heads. They found the note
undamaged in his mouth before they buried his charred
body.

The first radiotherapy session to help ease my mother's
back pains has begun. She tries to pretend that her mood is
better than before. The skin on her chest is riddled with

ulcers. She asks for the commode all the time now, as she can no longer get to the toilet. As she withers away, her depression worsens. She can no longer leave her bed, and her body's waste products can no longer leave her body. Sometimes a thin streak of blood trickles from her gums; she is hardly able to swallow her food. This morning a tune keeps repeating itself in my head—"Marquiza, Marquiza, Marquiza Caravaza," the theme song from a Russian children's cartoon film. They injected her with medication to decrease the level of calcium in her blood, which was the main cause of her pain. She hates the smell of women's perfume; it makes her nauseous. She says to me:

—I feel like a bag of old bones. My tongue is so dry, it feels as if it's coated in sand. Did you know that they've invented a new device which sprays medication into the mouth to moisten it? It's called artificial saliva.

She sprays a little into her mouth, adding:

—As for my back, they've advised me not to wash the area that's been treated. I'm not allowed to rub any oils or lotions into it, and I mustn't shave. It shouldn't be covered by clothing, exposed to sunlight or a cold breeze, and I mustn't rub ice on it. They gave me these instructions in a little booklet called, *Precautions for the coming months*. Ha! I get upset by the slightest sound. If somebody opens a paper wrapper near me, I lose my temper. How am I supposed to take precautions over the next few months?

I learned during this period how to listen to her. She would talk to me of her illness, her fears and her worries. The specter that haunted her days. Her weight is steadily dropping. Her awareness of her situation increases. She has

started wearing large sanitary pads to avoid the embarrassment of her unpredictable bowels. She laughs:

—You missed a sight to behold this morning. One of
the patients was unable to control herself. She dropped a
bucket of diarrhea on the floor. A puddle of filth; its stench
will linger in my nostrils for a week! But I'm smarter than
she is. They have allowed me to wear this continence pad.
What do you think? Isn't it a pretty color?

After a while, she remembers to add:

—By the way, did the professor tell you that both breasts
have now been completely invaded, and that the vertebrae
in the lower part of my back have been slowly eroded? They
now fear it might go to my liver.

When she talks, she looks like a helpless fish without
eyelashes.

—This is what I call English bluntness. They told me
that I might soon have difficulty lifting a glass of water.

—I will be here, Mother, don't worry.

—And now there is something new in my life: cyclizine
and co-proxamol. That awful smell of disinfectant ema-
nates from the nurses' pores!

She swallows a mouthful of water with some difficulty.

—How I wish I could go for a walk right now along the
riverfront. What ridiculous things we wish for, knowing
that we will never leave this place on our feet again.

After a while she adds:

—I feel the thought of God is getting nearer.

—Mother, God is not a thought.

—I dreamt that God was a short man, the size of a dwarf,
with a long white beard. He is waiting to document all my

sins in his big notebook. Do you think I will pass through Heaven's "Golden Gate"?

I smile at her:

—If God wishes.

She asks me if I remembered to switch off the gas under the pot of pasta she'd left on the stove. Probably six years ago!

The women on the ward walk about carrying bottles containing their fluids, yellow and red, which fill the plastic tubes that dangle from their breasts or abdomens or backs. A crumpled paper towel soaked in brown vomit lies in an aluminum container that has been placed by my mother's bedside. The skin at the angle of her mouth is cracked and fissured; she tries to swallow her painkillers. The antidepressants no longer work. The days in the hospital have become long hours that chew each other up. Her arms now resemble the thighs of a large turkey. She refuses to speak to the psychotherapists, declining their booklets about hope, coping with illness, how to deal with the urge to rebel, denial, and escaping from life. She says:

—If I were functioning normally, I would wipe my bottom with the paper from these booklets.

She draws a difficult breath.

The nights were no calmer than the days. I left her in the care of the nurses. I needed an hour of quiet for myself to prepare for the next day. I dreamed I was walking through the industrial area on the road to the Rasheed Military Camp. Nondescript mustard-colored buildings and cement blocks rise and fall, as one walled fence blends into another. The chain starts with the furniture factory belonging to

Shakir al-Najjar—"the carpenter," which was destroyed by fire a while ago. At the crossroads is Felah's car repair garage and Abu Haidar's shop, where they make feather pillows. Beside it is the stall selling lemon tea. I was looking for a farm where they sold the precious seeds of the yew trees. The locals told me to seek the man who ran the place, Hajji Abdul Zahra, a Muslim pilgrim returned from the hajj in the holy city, Mecca. However, he had emigrated to the north of the country, as the owner had been declared bankrupt. His address was not known.

9

A trail of transparent stickiness spread across the lower part of my abdomen, as if a wet snail wide as a fist had crawled across my belly. I hadn't known I was pregnant until six weeks after my last period—two weeks after Arnaud left for Kenya. He didn't contact me during the seventh week, so I had to make a decision on my own. I think of my mother. I tell myself every night that I must face my mistake before it's too late. I won't surrender as she did. I must resolve the situation. Sometimes, I wait for him to call, bursting into tears. Sometimes, I wait for the clinic appointment, worrying he might change my mind. I fall asleep by the telephone. I'm swallowed by a foggy passageway that leads me secretly to a sports hall, where other pregnant women are playing billiards. Their bellies hang over the green tables. They smoke. They're trying to concentrate on hitting the colored balls with the slender cue.

I enter the cavernous interior of a black cab on my way to the clinic. I remind myself that my mother has an appointment for another radiotherapy session this week. In the hall there is a queue of women and young girls with their mothers, waiting for the nurse to call out their names. The nurse is still at the reception desk, giving instructions to a patient over the phone:

—Yes, blood loss, contractions, and exhaustion—
She concludes her sentence:
—we believe a woman should listen to what her body is telling her. If you're tired, you should rest; if you're sleepy, you should lie down; and so on.
When she hangs up the phone, she turns to her colleague sitting behind the desk and says in a sarcastic tone:
—Hey, Anita, isn't it advice like that which got them pregnant in the first place?
Anita laughs:
—Yes, two-faced advice!
Fragments of noisy jazz music flow from a radio hidden away behind some drapes. The irregularity of the rhythm is irritating. I pull back the striped curtains. A warning note sits near the radio:

1. Please do not change the stations on this radio or switch it off.
2. This music has been chosen by a majority vote, as it is the most acceptable.
3. This station does not broadcast offensive material.
4. Switching off the radio might render the conversations in the nearby doctors' cubicles audible. This music acts as a barrier, the contravention of which would be a breach of the principles of trust and confidentiality upon which this service is based.
5. Thank you for your understanding.

My case is assigned to a Japanese lady doctor. I enter her office. She's wearing a white coat. Her shiny black hair has been arranged over the top of her head in a squarish cut. Her face looks like a white square surrounded by a black frame. She places my urine specimen on the desk, muttering:

—I don't know why they use the same foam cups for the urine samples as the ones they have in the cafeteria for the coffee!

She dons a rubber glove and asks me to get onto the examination table.

—Do you drink?

—No.

—Do you smoke?

—No.

—Drugs?

—No.

—Do you have any allergies?

—No.

—Have you ever been in hospital before in your life?

—No.

She smiles:

—What a boring patient you are! Anyway, a termination of pregnancy is a simple and rapid procedure. In the morning you come in; a few hours later you are discharged. You can go back to work the next day.

She prepares to take my blood. Behind her is a poster showing the segments of the uterus.

—You're not bothered by needles or the sight of blood?

—No, we often donated blood during the war.

—That explains your calm attitude.

When she'd taken the blood, she asks:

—Are you not ready for motherhood?

—I have no choice.

She nods her head:

—Yes, life is hard sometimes.

She picks up her pen. She has unintentionally knocked a sheet of contraceptive pills into her slippers, left by the side of her desk. She probably wears them when she's on call. She says in her academic tone:

—In your case, you have a threatened miscarriage.

She then reverts to her social tone:

—A girl of fourteen would be pleased to hear that statement. It would make her feel less guilty.

—I can understand that point of view.

—Anyway, a termination is indicated in your case.

Everything happens rapidly and efficiently. I wait for an hour in the cafeteria. I watch a child playing with a glass of light-colored fruit juice. He dips his biscuits in the drink; they crumble in his hands and sink to the depths in the form of starchy blobs. He enjoys his experiment and dips more biscuits in the juice till the biscuit box is empty. I imagine the biscuits are a fetus in a preservation solution. The hand of a man in his fifties rests on the table beside the child. I know those wrinkles well. I lift my eyes up to see his face, but in a blink he turns his back to me, heading out of the room. That hand was my father's.

After that, I find myself at the mercy of the Indian anesthetist. He reassures me that everything is alright. Before I float away from him, the Siluwa monster arrives. She orders me to spread my legs and, putting her head between my thighs, she starts to vacuum out my insides.

The nurses know the patients from the date of their last menstrual cycle. They move between the beds in the small ward handing out tampons, medication, and instructions for the days after the termination. The instructions advise not to swim in public swimming pools, not to participate in vigorous sports, and to refrain from sex for several weeks. I take my belongings and ask one of the nurses to get me a taxi.

I spend that night in the flat sweating between the sheets. Every now and then, I check the amount of blood loss, and I take the medication at the correct times. Arnaud has not contacted me yet. The four walls of the room entrap me, closing in from all sides. The room becomes as small as a matchbox. Strange hands have opened the box, burning its contents, matchstick after matchstick. My fate is like a matchbox—my side struck with pain, inside me a great emptiness. Is this what Anne was trying to describe when she talked about failing the Lord?

My mother has been moved to a single room so she can receive better care. When I get there the next morning, I can hear her screams as I enter the corridor. I rush up to see what has happened. The nurse stops me from entering the room. She tells me coolly:

—Slow down, young lady. There's nothing to worry about. We're merely trying to evacuate the waste products from her rectum manually because she no longer has the strength to do it the natural way. We don't want her to get blood poisoning. Of course, it is a very painful procedure, but I'm afraid there is no alternative.

When it is all over, I am allowed to enter my mother's room. She turns to look at me. Her face is white with exhaustion. She says:

—Damn this miserable life! No human being should have to go through this. I can no longer bear this physical degradation.

For the first time, my mother allowed me to hug her. She then put her head on my chest and wept bitterly.

Professor Karl speaks to me in the long white corridor.

—Your mother is now in the final stages. She is a sensitive woman, and she knows her time is approaching. We have allocated this private room to her so you can look after her emotionally. We will try to look after her medically, keeping her as comfortable as possible. I am sorry we were unable to stop the cancer from spreading; it has now reached her liver. You have to be strong for her sake. Until now, she has fought against it with exceptional bravery, refusing to accept strong sedatives.

He puts his hand on my shoulder, adding:

—I pray you will have strength and patience.

He turns around and heads toward the far end of the corridor, where the Department of Skin Diseases swallows his quiet footsteps.

My friend,

I thought I'd wait until the economic sanctions were lifted before writing to you. But we're now certain that that's not going to happen. The flowering gardenia tree in Jadria Street, from which we used to steal our share of blooms every spring, is sleeping underneath the rubble. The palm tree in my parents' garden has been struck by shrapnel from a nearby explosion. The prices of foodstuffs have become a nightmare. Everyone works merely to earn a mouthful of food, by any means. The

children outside the Passport Offices in the 52nd
District sell banana-flavored chewing gum. Those
outside the courts in the Karada area sell drinking
yoghurt. The magistrate on her way home warns them
about the dangers of typhoid fever. Less prosperous
children sell water.

The hot weather has become unbearable. The sun is
vertical; the blanket of heat melts even the stones. I
imagine humans are dissolving slowly. Each person
becomes a puddle, replacing the small shadows formed
by their erect figures a short while ago, on the pavement below their feet. The price of a kilo of dates is
unbelievable. Young men discuss the rise and fall in the
value of the dollar on the local black market. Young
women talk about the price of gold.

The number of pages in the newspapers is shrinking.
Arab Horizons magazine has ceased to exist. The only
use for the pages of *Alef Ba* magazine these days is to
wrap falafel sandwiches to prevent the grease from
soiling one's fingers; that's only because it's still being
printed on glossy paper.

Our relationship with the West is similar to the
physics theory of water reaching the same height in a
series of interconnected, parallel beakers. Whenever a
western delegation arrives, the beakers are moved; the
water dances to the right and to the left in agitation. But
when it is left alone, no matter how high or low the
beakers are, large or small, long or wide, the water
balances out, still and motionless. It submits to its
containers, lying on its back. You, my friend, are ahead
of us in time—we're only ahead of you in timing.

Farouk is mourning the death of his younger brother in an explosion in the Saydiya region. I wish your mother a speedy recovery.

Her letters were brief. Her words usually lined themselves up behind two teams, made up of "You" and "Us." The distance between them was now clearer than it had been in the past.

The hands on the clock are molten; the furniture in the room is changing—like a painting by Salvador Dali. The walls are pink. I still feel tired. I watch her laid out. The morphine is slowly paralyzing her. She's fighting in her sleep; her involuntary movements make her limbs jump suddenly beneath the covers, a minor spasm of muscles. Focusing, I try to memorize her features as they are. From which orifice will her soul leave her body? The mouth, the ear, the nose, or the vagina? My mother sleeps; she startles slightly and awakes. She asks me what time it is, and then she sleeps again.

At last, Arnaud comes to visit me at the hospital. We go down together to the cafeteria. He kisses me with some coolness. I ask him:

—Why didn't you get in touch?

—I'm sorry. The situation in Kenya has been difficult.

—I waited for you a long time. My news is not encouraging.

—I realize your mother isn't well.

—This has nothing to do with her.

I feel the coffee rising to my head. I say:

—When I asked for you in the Reptiles' Corner, they told me you'd left the flat.

—Yes, I was no longer getting any satisfaction from teaching the children at the Charles de Gaulle School. I needed a major change in my life.

—I thought I was about to change your life for you, but I was forced to act on my own.

—Are you serious? Are you trying to tell me you want to end our relationship?

—No, I'm trying to tell you I was pregnant!

He's taken aback. He fiddles with his collar:

—What?

He sinks into a lengthy silence.

I adopt my mother's sarcastic tone:

—Don't tell me you love children!

—I'm sorry, I'm really sorry. No, it's not a question of loving children. I—I don't know what to say. I hadn't realized. How can I explain to you how sorry I am, my God!

—You're getting worked up over nothing. It's been dealt with. I'm not waiting for a response from you. I merely wanted to discuss the issue with you.

—How calm you are! I'm so embarrassed. How did you go through this on your own?

—It doesn't matter how! The important thing is that I did!

—I never thought. . . . Actually, I never gave our affair enough consideration.

—I never expected any more of you. It's the age of confusion. Didn't we agree about that from the first day we met?

—My God, I feel like a pig. I never even told you I was married.

—Ha, I thought as much when you disappeared without any warning!

—No, please understand me, it doesn't mean I'm happy or anything of the sort. We're about to get divorced, but my wife is African, like my mother; their divorce laws have caught me in a trap.

—You don't owe me any explanations. I don't care if you were in Africa or on the moon. You could've been honest with me from the start. Anyway, it doesn't matter. We're aliens, and we shall part as aliens.

I add:

—Reptiles, in every sense of the word.

—Please don't! I don't want this to be an ordinary scenario from the life of two boring people. You mean so much more to me.

—I no longer wish to pay the price for both you and for myself.

—So is this a goodbye, or what?

I laugh:

—It's a what!

At this point he shouts in genuine anger:

—At least let me make it up to you!

I look at him for a moment and say:

—I think the problem in our relationship is that the problems we have are different.

I then add as I head toward the lifts:

—If you'll excuse me, I have a mother on the sixth floor who might be dying.

I leave behind me a Reptile metamorphosing into a pig.

· · ·

Entering my mother's room has become a burden in itself. I can no longer bear to watch her for more than fifteen minutes at a time. I start choking as I weep quietly. The nurses pat me on the shoulder as they enter and leave the room. I'm always holding a copy of the Koran in my hands. She moans and whimpers. Every now and then she utters a word of pain. She is now a skeleton lying in the bed, propped up with pillows on either side. Her dose of morphine increases every day, easing the pain of her final hours. When she rouses briefly from her coma, she asks for me, then says, "What time is it?" Her fingers are as weak as butter. She fights the cancer, yet succumbs slowly to the sedative, in a cruel game of snoozing and waking, until she slips away completely. I remember my father telling me once that the sense of hearing is the last to be lost as death approaches. I bring my lips close to her ear, "Mother, you're in the hands of the angels; don't worry about me. Let them take you to the safe place, where God is." She lets out a long resigned sigh.

At ten o'clock in the evening, her face contorts for several minutes. Her breathing becomes labored in a frightening way. Her heart rate drops. I exchange glances with the nurse, who nods back at me affirmatively. I hold her hand and wait. The rattling sound fills the room for several minutes; it seems as though my entire life had been lived during those moments. Finally she closes her exhausted eyelids.

I look at her . . . her skin is whiter than ever . . . around her eyes, her wrinkles are lax, like fine slivers of grated coconut left out for several days in yellow air.

10

Janet, Diane, and Jo-Jo come to visit me, carrying three modest bouquets of forlorn flowers. Many weeks of solitude pass by in the flat. I spend my time rearranging it. I add some plants in the corners. I've repainted the walls and mended a few things in the kitchen.

I got the job at the translation bureau and work from nine in the morning till five in the afternoon. My life revolves around my work, television in the evening, and opening the mail in the morning with a cup of bitter coffee.

Another autumn. My thirtieth year is nearing its end.

Madame's ruminating letters have become more infrequent. Events in my homeland are no longer considered newsworthy by the world's radio stations.

I remember from my last telephone conversation with her, when she had contacted me after a lengthy silence, the way she said Farouk had described the continuing sanctions, "We're eating shit with a needle; the needle doesn't pick anything up, and the pile of shit doesn't get any smaller!"

I wait for the No. 27 bus heading toward Kensington.

ACKNOWLEDGMENTS

Raneen Khedairi shared my childhood; I thank her for being my sister, and for his support I thank my brother-in-law, Dr. Omar Sammaraiee.

From Iraq, I would like to thank Dr. Muhannad Younis, Dr. Mehdi Hammadi, Dr. Alaa Tahir, and A. R. A. Wahid, for seeing a writer between the lines.

From Jordan, I am most grateful to Dr. Layla Naeem, Dr. Fehmi Jedaane, Mahir Kayali, and Atta Abdul Wahab for their efforts in publishing my book in Arabic.

My appreciation goes to Dr. Fadia Faqir, Toby Eady, and Deborah Garrison for their help in publishing the English edition. I also thank Marguerita Wilson for polishing the text.

I would also like to thank my cousins, Dr. Muhayman Jamil, for translating my book, and Manar Jamil, for revising it step by step.

Finally, my friends from Baghdad: They were my inspiration for a dream come true.

ABOUT THE AUTHOR

Betool Khedairi was born in Baghdad in 1965 to an Iraqi father and Scottish mother. She currently lives in Jordan. This is her first novel.